MISHAPS &
MEMORIES

A NOVELLA

MISHAPS & MEMORIES

A NOVELLA

PARADIGM
PRESS

MARTHA KEYES

CHAPTER ONE

T he value of a large, well-placed plant in a drawing room could not be overstated, for it was in just such a place that a man seeking to escape an unpleasant encounter might hide himself for a short time. Though *hide* was not the word James Carlisle would have preferred to use. He was merely sipping his champagne in solitude at his leisure, leaning against the wall, which just so happened to be concealed by an obliging plant.

"There you are." The frowning face of James's father, Henry Carlisle, appeared. "What in heaven's name are you doing in the corner of the room, hiding behind a tree?" He brushed at a few protruding leaves with an impatient hand.

James finished off what was left in his glass and stood straight. "I am not *hiding*, Father."

His father scoffed lightly. "Then what *are* you doing?"

James's mouth turned down in a frown as he contemplated his response. "I am"—he stroked a leaf with a finger —"enjoying nature."

"What you *should* be doing is asking Miss Garrett to dance."

James had made sure to remain in his corner until Miss Garrett was engaged for this set. Through the leaves of the tree, he could see her performing the beginning figures of a cotillion on the ballroom floor. "She appears to be well-entertained without my interference."

"My point precisely," his father said testily. "At this rate, she will have three offers of marriage before you have even emerged from this ridiculous corner." He swatted the leaves that sat against his shoulder. "Sir William leaves in the morning for his estate, and he shall be gone a fortnight, after which he will be paying Miss Garrett's father a visit. All you need do is exert yourself a little in the meantime— snatch her up before he does."

"I have never been terribly fond of *snatching*, as you so elegantly phrase it, Father."

His father's lips drew into a thin line. "I am running out of patience for your aversion to marriage, James. What reason can you possibly have to be so set against it?"

James stepped away momentarily to set his glass on the tray of the passing footman, biting his tongue as he did so. He didn't have an aversion to marriage, and he was not set against it. But he didn't particularly care to explain to his father why he was reluctant to offer for someone like Miss Garrett. His father would have no patience for the sentimentality that made James wish for something more than a practical match.

"It is merely the joy you take in defying me, no doubt," his father said with obvious resentment.

James smiled sardonically. "How well you know me, Father."

His father's frown deepened, and he glanced around at the chattering crowds lining the ballroom floor. "You could have the pick of the young women here—no doubt half a dozen of them came here with the express hope of being asked to dance by you—but instead, I find you paying your addresses to a . . . a *fern!*"

James frowned. "That is not fair, Father. I would never pay my addresses to a common fern. I am tolerably certain this is a fig tree."

His father was not amused. "Your mother and I wish to see you settled. Prosperous!"

James offered no response to this.

"Bah!" his father grumbled. "You never did care for anyone's wishes but your own. But mark my words, James. You *will* marry. And since you refuse to choose a bride, I have taken the liberty of choosing one for you." And with that, he turned on his heel.

James's smile faded as he watched his father disappear amongst the crowds. James *did* care what his parents thought. He merely wished that their desire for his prosperity was centered more on his happiness than on his marrying well.

Perhaps James was foolish to hope for more than a

strategic marriage. Perhaps only the most fortunate managed to marry for more than necessity. Surely, that opportunity would have presented itself already after so many years of being introduced to the Season's most promising and highly regarded young ladies.

Thinking perhaps it had been a mistake after all to attend tonight's dinner, James emerged from his corner, only to be confronted by his friend, Philip Langham.

"Your father said I would find you here." Langham peered around James, as though he expected to see someone behind the tree. "Thought he might snap my head off just for asking."

"I am in his black books," James said.

"Have you ever been out of them?"

James cocked his head to the side, frowning. "Not that I know of. Tonight, he finds me too lazy on the subject of marriage—and Miss Garrett. He insists I come up to scratch and—how did he phrase it?—*snatch her up* before Sir William manages to." James's gaze traveled to Miss Garrett again, only to find that, despite being engaged in conversation with Mr. Coombs, her eyes were on him.

"Miss Garrett?" Langham said with a hint of distaste. "The one who stares?"

James held Miss Garrett's gaze, but as she showed no sign of embarrassment at being caught in the act of looking at him, and because he found her gaze particularly unnerving, he admitted defeat and looked away first. "Yes, the one who stares. But what is the inconsequential habit of gawking in comparison with her father's barony?"

"I don't know, Carlisle," Langham said incredulously. "I imagine you would find it consequential enough if you found her forever staring at you when you were trying to read *The Times* in peace at the breakfast table."

James suppressed a shudder.

"Just so," Langham said. "Her entire family has a strange kick to their gallop. Her sister married that devilish poor fellow from Yorkshire. They won't hear a word against him, though. Nothing more certain to set up their hackles than maligning the working class. I tell you what, Carlisle. Your problem is that you are too charming by half. You must take a leaf from Miss Garrett's book and acquire some undignified habit—an obscenely loud laugh or perhaps pretending to be hard of hearing. If you would but set your mind to it, it would be easy enough to give her a reason to prefer Sir William."

James cursed under his breath. His parents were approaching, with Miss Garrett and her father at their side.

"Gads," Langham said as his eyes followed James's gaze. "One would think she would have to blink every now and then. What a lovely evening you have ahead of you, Carlisle. I understand all of the courses are to be fish, too."

James's head whipped around, looking in vain for any sign that his friend was joking. But Langham only gave a sympathetic grimace.

"Our dear host wished to pay tribute to the sea before he leaves back to Shropshire for the summer."

James stifled a groan. Coming this evening had decidedly been a mistake. He couldn't abide fish—not since he'd become violently ill after eating some as a child.

"For someone who so enjoys being in a boat on the water, your hatred of the fish that dwell in that water is quite ironic."

"I am aware of that," James said, unamused.

Insensitive to his friend's predicament, Langham slapped James on the back and strode off.

Miss Garrett's eyes were still on James—though, to be completely fair, so were those of his parents and Lord Linscott—and he pasted on a smile to receive them.

"Ah, son," his father said, the pleasant expression on his face giving no indication of the bad terms they had parted on just minutes ago. "I was just telling Lord Linscott how anxious you are to pay him a visit. He and Miss Garrett said they would be happy to receive you once they are settled back in at Linscott House. What date was it you said, my lord?"

Lord Linscott inclined his head. "I believe it was the twentieth. If it is convenient to you, of course."

James could feel Miss Garrett's unblinking eyes boring into him with even more power than usual. Did they never become dry? He opened his mouth to express his regrets at not being able to agree to the date in question, but his father spoke over him.

"Yes, yes. The twentieth will do perfectly, won't it, James? And now, I believe they are about to ring the bell. You will, of course, take Miss Garrett in to dinner, son."

James smiled through gritted teeth and offered Miss Garrett his arm. "Of course, Father."

Perhaps it was time to see just how willing the young woman was to look past his faults—or stare past them, rather.

CHAPTER TWO

Judith Jardine pushed on the fabric at the fingertips of her borrowed gloves, hoping to force them farther down. Anne's fingers were much longer than hers—and much more elegant, certainly. Only when she had seen Anne's hands deftly working a needle earlier that day had Judith realized how coarse her own hands were in comparison. She was glad they would be covered—until dinner, of course. She must simply hope that people would be too focused on eating to notice.

The glow of the ballroom ahead spilled out of the doors and into the candlelit corridor, the music along with it. The smell of violets swept by as a young couple brushed past, arm-in-arm, with laughter on their lips.

Judith's cousin, Anne Dawes, patted Judith's arm with a smile full of eagerness. "You must leave the gloves be, Judy. No one shall take notice if they are a little long. Not when you are looking so ravishing." She nudged Judith with a teasing elbow.

Heat seeped into Judith's cheeks, and she shot Anne an annoyed look. She had never been to such a fine gathering, and she was sorely conscious of how little she belonged, from her drooping gloves and unpolished hands to her ill-fitting gown.

"This is your chance," Anne whispered excitedly. "I am so thrilled your father agreed to let you come. A week is not terribly long, I admit, but I am very hopeful we shall find someone for you."

"Oh, hush, Anne," Judith said. "Our efforts are better spent finding someone for *you*. Just being here is reward enough for me. Besides, no one here would seriously consider marrying someone like me."

She said the words as much for her own benefit as for Anne's. She couldn't deny that her hopes were high for this short visit in Brighton. Never again was the opportunity to rub shoulders with so many eligible gentlemen likely to come her way—not as the daughter of a country vicar. It had been a difficult enough task to receive permission from him to come—he worried about her head being turned by such frivolity and that she would return home with a dissatisfaction for her life.

And perhaps he was right. As Anne and her mother introduced Judith to person after person, she could see their evaluative gazes taking her in and the subsequent approbation in their eyes as she made her curtsies and greeted everyone the way her mother had taught her.

Anne was delighted with Judith's success, and Judith felt both relief and pleasure, tempered only with the suspicion that everyone's interest and esteem would flounder when they came to know of her family's reduced circumstances.

"Given how things are going tonight," Anne said with a squeeze to Judith's arm, "a week will be more than enough time to secure the interest of *several* gentlemen." She was more than happy to spend the time between introductions making Judith acquainted with the eligibility of the gentlemen in the ballroom, starting on one end and moving toward the other.

Judith secretly made note when Anne mentioned men of respectable stock who were neither titled nor particularly wealthy. If Judith had any chance of success, it would certainly be with them and not the barons and sons of nabobs in attendance.

"And *that*"—with a nod of the head, Anne indicated the corner of the room where a group of a few people stood—"is the one and only Mr. James Carlisle."

Judith's gaze took in three older people and a beautiful young woman, finally settling on a younger gentleman. He stood one dark-haired head above the others, and though he was inarguably handsome and his smile charming, the latter had a pasted-on look about it.

"The most sought-after gentleman in attendance, I think," Anne said, obvious admiration in her eyes.

"More so than the viscount you mentioned?"

"Well, I suppose it depends on whether you wish for a

man with a title empty of money, a disagreeable appearance, and the awful habit of winking *or,*" Anne said, her head tilting to the side as she admired Mr. Carlisle, "a man with an obscenely large fortune—made in the East Indies, mind you, but that unfortunate fact we can easily overlook —a baron for an uncle, and the most pleasing face you ever did look upon. Not that it matters. I understand he and Miss Garrett are intended for one another. She is the one he is speaking with."

Judith didn't disagree with her cousin's assessment of either man, but neither of them were worth a second thought. Not for her, at least. Anne might have some hope with a viscount or a man like Mr. Carlisle, but for her part, Judith would happily settle for a young man who could give her a few new dresses each year and put a smile on her face.

Two such men had already stood out this evening, and both had shown clear interest in Judith upon their introduction. She had great hopes that she would enjoy a set with both after dinner—perhaps she would even be seated next to them if she was fortunate—where she would have the opportunity to gauge just how genuine their interest in her was.

But fortune chose not to smile on her in such a way. In fact, it seemed to frown heavily upon her, since she found herself seated at the very far end of the table, with Anne across from her, Mr. Carlisle to her right, and no companion to her left. What a waste of a perfectly good opportunity to continue her acquaintance with Mr. Brown or Mr. Doyle.

Judith sighed and resigned herself to the situation. Had she not told Anne that simply being here was reward enough?

Her eyes fell upon the host of dishes covering every inch of the dining room table, and they widened in dismay. She had anticipated they would be served by footmen, but apparently the hostess preferred to have the guests serve one another. She swallowed down her silly fear. She would not be the one doing the serving, at least. Mr. Carlisle would be expected to perform that task.

Whether he forgot about her or was simply too occupied with responding to Miss Garnett's continuous flow of conversation on his other side, Judith couldn't be certain. Whatever the reason, she was obliged to either starve or serve herself more often than not, and even when Mr. Carlisle *did* turn to ask whether she desired a particular dish, it was with a look of such distaste on his lips that Judith couldn't help but color up and wonder whether perhaps he'd had word of her ineligibility and was disgusted to be seated beside her. At least he would not notice the coarse state of her hands when he could barely spare a glance in her direction.

Anne sent Judith frequent, significant looks, prodding her to engage Mr. Carlisle in conversation. But Judith could see no purpose in such an endeavor, nor had the two of them been introduced properly. It was highly awkward.

"I admit I was glad to hear of the match between

them," Miss Garrett said loud enough that those around could hear. Her eyes were locked on Mr. Carlisle, wide and blue, as though she couldn't bear to look elsewhere.

"Oh," Mr. Carlisle responded in a voice just as loud, "but for him to marry so far below his station cannot but offend finer sensibilities. Good breeding cannot be bought, of course, but it does go hand-in-hand with money."

Judith clenched her jaw. What an insufferable man! Be he ever so good-looking, he did *not* deserve that so many young women should be wishing for his attention.

At one point during the second course, there seemed to be a lull in the conversation between him and Miss Garrett, and to Judith's surprise, he turned toward her. However attractive she had found him in the ballroom, the look of exasperation he wore as he faced her—as if she was an intolerable obligation—drained him of any appeal to her.

He held a plate of fish in his hands. "Would you care for any, Miss—" He frowned.

"Jardine," Judith said. "And yes, please. Just a bit of the sardines, if you would be so kind." That he had already forgotten her name from the first time she had relayed it to him said more than enough about him. How he presumed to speak about good breeding when he showed so little himself was beyond her. If this was what people of the *ton* were like, she was glad not to be counted one of them.

Mr. Carlisle served her from the platter with the same look of distaste he had worn whenever he turned to her, and with hot cheeks, she noted his eyes flick to her hands as she held her plate at the ready to receive the food. But when he looked to set the platter down, there was no room for it—the gentleman across from him had set a plate of salmon in its place.

"Oh, here." Judith reached for the platter he held. There was a large enough spot for it at her end of the table. But Mr. Carlisle had not heard her. Her attempt to take the dish surprised him, and he pulled it back toward himself. The platter tipped, spilling three sardines and their juices onto his lap.

Mr. Carlisle jumped up from his chair in a failed effort to avoid the spill, and Judith's eyes widened in horror at the sight of his soiled breeches and waistcoat.

His face screwed up as all gazes turned to him, and he let out a frustrated gush of air from his nose.

"Thank you, Miss Jardine," he said with an ironic smile. "Or was it Miss *Sardine*?"

There was a veritable fire blazing on Judith's cheeks as chuckles rippled around the table at the pun.

Mr. Carlisle brushed at the spill with his napkin, but the smell of sardines filled the air around him, and he tossed down the cloth onto the table with a resigned sigh.

"If you will excuse me." He bowed and left the room, which teemed with light laughter, punctuated by the words, "Miss Sardine."

CHAPTER THREE

Bucket in hand, Judith walked the path that led from her sister Mary's house to the beach. She could see the coastline, stretching west toward Eastbourne and Brighton. The water shimmered, reminding her momentarily of the dress she had worn to her first real ball. What a disaster.

She looked away, refusing to acknowledge the warmth the memory brought about. She had been foolish to think a week amongst the set who frequented such a ball would amount to anything.

If the week there had been a foray into a new, glittering world, her arrival at her sister's seaside cottage had been the equivalent of a slap in the face. Mary and George Bradford's home and circumstances were even more humble than those of Judith's family, and when Judith had arrived yesterday, it was just as the sole maid, Jane, had been leaving—dismissed for theft.

The sound of giggling brought Judith's head around. Three young girls stood in front of the small house next to the path, their heads together.

"Miss Sardine!" one called. More giggles ensued.

Judith's eyes widened momentarily. She gave a pretend smile and turned her head away with a clenched jaw. They were only children, but that didn't make the words any less unwelcome. She had sincerely hoped that, in leaving Brighton, she would also leave behind the nickname that had dogged her entire week there.

Apparently that had been too much to hope for. Mary must have told one of the neighbors of Judith's unfortunate experience, and in a small place like Portsbury, word always spread like a fire in a field of dry crops.

Father had been worried at the effect of Judith's Brighton visit on her pride. Well, his worry had never been so unwarranted. She doubted she had any left to her.

She let out an irritable sigh as she kneeled down next to the small stream that emptied into the ocean, dipping the dirty bucket to clean it of the grimy water inside from scrubbing the hearth. She looked out to the beach wistfully. She had known her time in Portsbury would be full of tasks—she was here to help Mary before her confinement, after all—but she had not been prepared to take on the work of a maid as well. She had envisioned at least a few walks on the beach.

The waves lapped up against rocks and boulders of varying sizes, their bases covered in thick moss. The water was rougher than usual today. A small boat knocked against the rocks with each incoming surge. She squinted at a heap of clothing on the sand as the foamy fringe of a wave gathered around it. Her eyes widened, and she hurried up from her knees, dropping the bucket and running toward the heap. It was no pile of clothing—it was a person.

She lifted her skirts as her feet kicked up damp sand. Whether the man was dead or simply unconscious, she didn't know, but her heart hammered against her chest as she came up beside him. A wave approached, and, over-coming her fright at the sight that might await her, she pulled on the man's shoulder to bring him from his side to his back—and his face away from the approaching water.

He slumped onto his back, head lolling at an uncom-fortable angle. Judith stilled.

It couldn't be. She blinked, then searched the face of the man before her—the man who had dubbed her "Miss Sardine," who had looked at her with disgust, who had ruined her chances of a match. It was Mr. Carlisle. The prig.

A wet chill seeped into Judith's boots, and she sucked in a breath of surprise, tearing her eyes away from Mr. Carlisle to note the gathering water. She took both of his arms and pulled with all her might, so that his body slid away from the water and onto the sand the waves hadn't yet reached.

Panting, she kneeled down beside him. Was he alive? His face had plenty of color, and his eyes were closed—thank the heavens for that.

"Mr. Carlisle," she said softly. There was no response.

"Mr. Carlisle," she said more loudly. Still nothing.

What could she do? She looked at the state of him—dirt, seaweed, and moss covered his clothing. Her gaze moved to his unbuttoned waistcoat and the sopping shirt beneath, plastered to his skin. Her lips drew into a thin line, but she lowered her ear to listen.

It was there—a soft heartbeat—and she breathed more freely. He was alive, at least.

But now what? How was she to wake him from this state?

She had once seen a senseless, drunken man slapped to consciousness. It was certainly tempting.

But, no.

Instead, she put a hand to his cheek and said his name as loud as she could without shouting. It was no use, though. He would have to be carried, and she certainly wasn't strong enough to do it.

❦

MR. CARLISLE SHOWED SIGNS OF STIRRING AS MARY'S neighbor, Mr. Barry, brought him into the house, heaving from the effort of carrying such a load. He had been obliged to stop more than once to rest. After a moment of consideration inside Mary's house, Judith instructed that Mr. Carlisle be set down in her own bed. He would need to be seen to, and it would be easiest there.

On more than one occasion during the last week, she

had considered what she would say to Mr. Carlisle if she were ever to see him again. None of the things she had come up with were civil enough to be uttered aloud, but that was just as well, for she'd had no anticipation of the opportunity presenting itself. It most certainly hadn't occurred to her that she would be offering up her own bed to him.

She thanked Mr. Barry, asking him to see that the surgeon was called for, and Mary entered soon after, a hand on her round belly and questions pouring forth. But there was no time to explain anything. Mr. Carlisle was coming to.

He groaned softly and reached a hand to the crown of his head, wincing. The fingers came away red.

"You've injured your head," Judith said. She hadn't noticed the blood until now, hidden as it was amongst his drying hair.

He blinked rapidly, eyes fixed on her as though trying to bring her into focus.

She waited for any glimmer of recognition, but recognition never appeared. Of course, he didn't remember her —the pompous pig had hardly glanced in her direction at the dinner.

His gaze flickered around the room—small, cramped, and bare of furnishing as it was. "What is this place?"

Judith had been wrong. She *did* have a bit of pride left in her, and the dismay in both his expression and voice as he took in his surroundings fanned the flame bright. He was horrified by where he found himself.

"You are in Portsbury," Judith said in a clipped voice.

"Portsbury," Mr. Carlisle repeated softly, forehead drawn into a deep frown. "Do I live here?"

Judith glanced at Mary, but Mary had no idea who this man was. Did Mr. Carlisle truly not remember?

"Do you know your name, sir?" Judith asked.

Mr. Carlisle's gaze was fixed on her, though he seemed not to be truly looking at her. "I . . . I . . ." He put a hand to his head again. "What happened? Who are you?"

Part of Judith felt bad for Mr. Carlisle. But another part of her wanted the first thing he remembered to be how terrible he had been to her. His memory would undoubtedly return to him once he'd had some time, but for just a moment, she wanted him to know what it felt like not to be the most desired and eligible bachelor. How fitting it would be for the tables to turn—for someone as insufferable as the dashing Mr. James Carlisle to wake, finding himself in just the sort of life and lowly station he had deplored at dinner.

She spoke before she could think better of it. "You were out fishing for sardines."

She watched him, ignoring the way Mary tilted her head to the side with her questioning gaze on Judith.

"I was fishing?"

Judith nodded, nostrils flared, enjoying the confusion in Mr. Carlisle's expression. "You must have been knocked over by a wave—they are frightfully large today. I hope this doesn't mean you shan't be able to carry out your duties."

"Duties?"

Judith donned her most innocent, wide-eyed expression. "Yes, duties." She gave a little laugh. "Oh dear. Has your injury truly made you forget everything? I *have* heard that a blow to the head can do strange things."

Mr. Carlisle rubbed at his forehead with a hand. "Forgive me—I find my brain is very muddled—but am I a *servant?*"

Judith did her best to suppress a smile, blinking. "Why, but of course! You have served here for two years now. Ow!" A forceful hand squeezed Judith on the shoulder, and she whipped around to look at Mary, who stood behind her, a significant and unamused expression on her face. Judith felt a pang of guilt at her sister's expression.

"Might I have a word with you, Judith dearest?" Mary asked through clenched teeth.

Judith rose reluctantly and allowed her sister to pull her into the short, dark corridor.

"What in heaven's name are you doing?" Mary hissed, gripping Judith's arm tightly.

Judith pulled it from her grasp. "Making the world a more just place! If only for a few glorious minutes."

"How in the world is telling such a lie justice for that poor, injured man?"

Judith scoffed. "Oh, don't tell me you have become a victim to his beautiful face as well."

"What on earth are you talking about, Judy? What has his face got to do with anything?"

Judith leaned in closer to ensure her voice could not

be heard in the bedroom. "Do you know who that is, Mary?"

"I have never seen him in my life."

Judith smiled with faux-sweetness. "Well, *Miss Sardine* has."

Mary stared at her, then glanced at the gap in the door, where Mr. Carlisle could be seen staring blankly at the wall. "*That* is him?"

"It is. The very *gentleman* himself."

Mary said nothing for a moment, still staring at Mr. Carlisle. Finally, she looked to Judith. "But you cannot seriously mean to persuade him that he is our servant, Judith. That is utter madness."

"It is a bit of harmless fun, Mary. He has hit his head. He will regain his memories before Mr. Sharp arrives, and perhaps he will learn a valuable lesson in the meantime."

Mary shot her a severe look. "Or perhaps you will ruin your reputation for the sake of some silly attempt at retribution."

"Reputation?" Judith gave a caustic laugh. "What reputation? I am known now as *Miss Sardine*, even here in Portsbury, thanks to that man. Any hope I had of securing a match was ruined when he made me into the joke of Brighton Society." She took in a deep breath, trying to calm herself. "I will tell him the truth, Mary. You needn't worry. Only let me have a moment to enjoy the world as it should be. Heaven knows men like him could use a little dose of humility."

Mary held Judith's gaze silently. A baby's cry sounded

in the next room, and Mary sighed. "You will do as you please, Judy. You always do. But I will play no part in it. I must go get Charlie now." She gave Judith a final, sober look, then made her way to her bedroom.

Judith stood in the corridor for a moment, eyes on the gap in the door and Mr. Carlisle within. She hated knowing Mary disapproved of her behavior, but Mary had not been there for the continuous teasing—harmless as it may have seemed to those engaging in it—that Judith had experienced while in Brighton. No one had been able to take her seriously after Mr. Carlisle's mockery.

Judith's jaw tightened, and she stepped back into her bedroom, where Mr. Carlisle had begun to shiver.

CHAPTER FOUR

James clenched his eyes shut, straining at his name, a memory, at anything to help ground him and tell him this was not a dream.

The door creaked, and he opened his eyes. The same young woman appeared who had been sitting next to him. The hem of her dress was wet, and her soft brown hair, though tied back in a bun high on her head, had come loose in places, falling onto her forehead and temples in a becoming way. James's pounding head hurt even more when he reminded himself that he was this young woman's servant.

"I am very sorry," he said apologetically, "but along with my own name, I seem to have forgotten yours. Well, everyone's, really. But I should know the name of my mistress." The words sounded strange on his lips. But *all of this* felt strange. He had no recognition whatsoever of this room nor the two women he had seen since waking from the accident—while fishing for sardines, evidently.

She reached for a blanket in the corner and brought it over to the bed. "Oh, I am not your mistress. That would be my sister, Mary. Mary Bradford. Her husband, George, is away right now, I'm afraid, which makes the timing of your accident all the more lamentable."

"Indeed," he said. "How should I address you, ma'am?"

She glanced at him with a frown, and there was a pause before her response. She almost looked displeased. Had he said something unacceptable? How could a man wake, able to speak, but with no more memory or knowledge than a newborn babe of how to go on with people he had been serving for years?

"It is miss. Miss Jardine," she finally said. She didn't move, gaze fixed on him watchfully.

He reached for the blanket as another shiver racked his body. "Thank you, Miss Jardine."

She put out a hand for the blanket. "We should change your clothing first, otherwise the blanket will not warm you for long."

He stared at her.

"*You*," she said, and her cheeks looked more pink than they had before. "You should change your clothing first. That is, if you are able. I can see whether Mr. Barry might come help you if you are in need of assistance."

"No," James said. "I can manage. Though, would you mind helping me up?"

Miss Jardine nodded curtly. Apparently, servants were not supposed to ask their superiors for help standing. He made mental note of the fact. How many blunders would he make as he tried to fulfill what was expected of him?

Miss Jardine came over to him and hesitated a moment before sitting beside him. She slipped her hands behind his back to push him up from his lying position. He felt weak, but she pushed him forward with more strength than he had anticipated. He shifted his legs so that they swung over the edge of the bed, and Miss Jardine set his arm around her neck to help him to a stand. He kept a hand on the bed to stabilize himself, and she extracted herself from under his arm.

"Thank you, Miss Jardine," he said.

"I shall just go retrieve your clothing," she said, and she left the room.

He looked around and sighed. For some reason, the view depressed him.

Miss Jardine returned shortly with a pile of folded clothing in hand.

"Here," she said, setting the clothing on the bed. "Freshly laundered—by you, earlier today." She wore a smile on her face now—one that James could only describe as satisfied—and it enhanced her beauty. "I shall leave you to change. If you are in need of assistance, you need only call out. When you have finished, knock three times on the door to apprise me of it."

James nodded and picked up the trousers that sat on top of the clothing pile, sincerely hoping he wouldn't be obliged to call for Miss Jardine in the middle of changing them. He might have been overly confident in his assertion that he would need no assistance.

"Miss Jardine," he said as she reached the door.

She turned to look at him, and suddenly, he felt sheepish.

"What is my name?"

She didn't respond immediately. It was almost as if she was considering whether to respond at all. "James," she finally said.

There was a familiar ring to that, and he welcomed it gladly—a glimmer of hope that perhaps his memories were still intact somewhere inside his head.

He managed to peel the wet clothing from his skin and don the new ones without being obliged to call for help, but by the time he had finished, his head was pounding, and he had become aware of other injuries on his body. He stumbled over to the door, shutting his eyes against the pain, and rapped on it three times, making his way back to the bed, where he sat and waited.

Miss Jardine arrived shortly, but she stopped in the doorway at the sight of him, putting a hand to her mouth. It didn't quite cover the edges of her smile or the laughter in her eyes.

James followed her gaze down to his clothing and grimaced.

"It seems as though I lost half of my body along with all of my mind," he said with a rueful smile. His shirt hung loosely around him, and if not for the straps that held them up, his trousers would have fallen to the floor.

Miss Jardine stepped into the room, shutting the door behind her. "Yes, well, we have all slenderized a bit of late, what with our straitened circumstances. You more than anyone, though. Thankfully, it has made you quicker about your duties."

His duties. What *were* his duties? "I am sure this is all quite troublesome to you," he said, "but can you help me remember what exactly my duties are? You said I was fishing when I hit my head? And that I did the laundry earlier?"

"Yes," she said as she sat and smoothed the covers on the bed. "Before that, you had come from cleaning the privy, I believe."

James's eyes widened. "Cleaning the . . ."

Miss Jardine looked at him with a wide, clear gaze. "Yes, normally, you wake before sunrise to light the kitchen fire, sweep, prepare breakfast, of course, then on to the carpets and dusting. While we eat breakfast, you see to the beds, and—" She stopped. "Is there something wrong?"

James swallowed. "No, that is, well, it is just . . . one would think I would have some sort of memory of these things, but everything you are saying sounds so . . . foreign."

She patted his hand. "I am certain it will all come back to you as you carry out the tasks." Muffled voices sounded somewhere nearby, and she straightened. "I believe the surgeon has arrived. I will show him in."

James gave a reluctant nod as Miss Jardine went to the door. He didn't know whether to hope his memory returned or not.

CHAPTER FIVE

J udith shut the door to her bedroom and immediately covered her mouth with a hand to stop the irrepressible laughter that rose to her lips. The chagrin on Mr. Carlisle's face—the look of utter horror when she had mentioned the privy. It felt almost like justice had been served for the humiliation he had caused her. *Almost.*

She let out a sigh as she heard Mary greet the surgeon. The fun was over now. She had assured Mary she would tell Mr. Carlisle the truth, and she would be as good as her word once the surgeon saw to him. No doubt it was for the best. Judith couldn't deny the guilt that lurked behind her amusement. Mr. Carlisle *was* injured, after all, and to take advantage of that was not something she anticipated being proud of in retrospect.

Mr. Sharp stayed with Mr. Carlisle for a matter of ten minutes and, as Mary was occupied with Charlie, it fell to Judith to confer with him afterward. The surgeon was a man of somber demeanor, with thick, gray eyebrows that curled up at the top like the wings of a bird about to take flight. She tried to suppress her nerves at the somber look on his face. Did he know what she had done? Would he scold her?

He shook his head, a troubled expression on his face as Judith stood with him just outside the door to her room. "He seems to have lost all recollection of the past. Nary a memory left!"

Trying to conceal her relief and surprise, Judith shook her head soberly. "Very sad."

"I have seen cases like this before. A blow to the head is an unpredictable thing, and I urge you to take the utmost caution with him, Miss Jardine."

Judith swallowed and nodded quickly. "Of course."

"We must hope that his memories return, but they must do so at their own pace." He turned a severe eye on her. "You mustn't, on any account, force them upon him. It might overset him." He shook his head regretfully. "I once knew a woman in just such a situation. Her family attempted to remind her of her past."

Judith waited. To no avail. "And what was the result?"

"She died in Bethlem Hospital, raving mad."

Judith's eyes widened and her stomach dropped.

Mr. Sharp seemed content with her reaction, and the severity in his gaze lessened slightly. "I have great hope that his memories will return with time, but they must be coaxed out gently. Let him rest today, but do not leave him alone for long periods of time while he is so disoriented.

See to his wounds. Then, slowly but surely, encourage him to engage in the activities he was accustomed to before the unfortunate accident. *That* is the best method for assisting him in regaining normalcy."

Judith managed a nod, but she was beginning to feel sick inside. Mr. Sharp moved to walk toward the door, and she followed.

"I shall come check on him soon to see how he is getting along. We can reassess the situation then. Good day, Miss Jardine."

"Thank you," she said, hoping the panic building within her was not evident.

"Oh, Mr. Sharp!"

He turned toward her, bushy eyebrows sloping down in a frown.

"You said *wounds*," she said. "I was only aware of one —on his head."

"He received some cuts and bruises as well. I recommend replacing the strips and the salve with fresh ones in two hours or so. Good day."

Judith shut the door behind him and stared blankly at the wood grains on the door. What in heaven's name was she to do?

"Judy?"

She whipped around to find Mary looking at her, face full of concern. "What did Mr. Sharp say?"

Judith took in a large breath and grimaced.

CHAPTER SIX

Mary listened without saying a word as Judith recounted what the surgeon had said. When she had finished, Judith waited for the chastisement she knew she deserved. But she was treated instead to her sister's ill-suppressed amusement.

Judith frowned, waiting impatiently for her sister to gain control of herself.

"I am sorry," Mary said, still covering her mouth, "but you cannot deny it is diverting."

"Diverting?" Judith said incredulously.

Mary nodded, wiping at one of her eyes, which had begun to leak with her laughter.

"Do you not understand, Mary? I cannot tell him the truth now without the risk of condemning him to lunacy—or death."

Mary waved an impatient hand. "Mr. Sharp does so enjoy his dramatics."

Judith's brows knit. "So, you think I should tell Mr. Carlisle the truth?"

"No."

Judith let out a snort and folded her arms, waiting for her sister to expound on her contradictory remarks.

"You should follow Mr. Sharp's counsel, of course, but I expect Mr. Carlisle's memory shall return shortly on its own. After a night of good sleep, in all likelihood."

Judith chewed on her lip. She was trapped in a cage of her own making. "*This* is what comes of trying to help people."

Mary raised a brow.

"What?" Judith said defensively. "I could have left him on the beach. Someone else would no doubt have come upon him, and then *they* would be saddled with his care."

"And were you trying to *help* Mr. Carlisle when you informed him he was a servant here?"

"Yes," Judith said, lifting her chin. "For what could help an insufferably proud person more than to give them a dose of humility? It was for his own good."

Mary gave a decisive nod. "No doubt. And now, as a result, *you* have learned a lesson about the dangers of telling falsehoods, however justified or well-meaning they may be. I simply find a bit of amusement in the predicament you have created for yourself. May it be of great benefit to both of you in the end."

Judith gave a snort. "What, then, do you propose, *sister dearest*? Mr. Sharp instructed that Mr. Carlisle slowly engage in the activities he was accustomed to before his accident. Perhaps you failed to notice, but I am not the most fit person to chaperon a man to balls and dinner parties—or whatever it is he spends his time doing."

"No, of course not." Mary shrugged her shoulders. "You said yourself that some humility would benefit the man. If he believes himself to be my servant, then, by all means, let him see what it means to be a servant."

"Mary!" Judith cried. "You cannot be serious."

"It shan't harm him. We certainly could use the help until we find someone to replace Jane, and I cannot do that until George returns. Besides, the presence of a strong man in the household will let *me* sleep more soundly. The Barrys had a window broken and their silverware stolen the other night."

Judith said nothing, staring down the corridor at the bedroom door and chewing on the tip of her thumb. They *did* need help, even if it was something as simple as watching Charlie or helping with washing up after dinner. Mary needed rest if she was to keep the baby in until George returned in ten days.

Mary nudged her. "A bit of lowly work may coax the memories out of him more quickly than lazing around at some club would do. Every bone in his body will revolt at being made to do such work if he is the sort of man you've described."

Judith smiled slightly. *That* was also true. What was the wording Mr. Carlisle had used? *For him to marry so far below his station cannot but offend finer sensibilities.* Yes, well, perhaps the offense of living below his station would help him remember his own fine sensibilities.

With Charlie in Judith's arms, she and Mary went to Mr. Carlisle. He was lying back on the bed, head bandaged and eyes closed, but they opened with the creaking of the door.

Together, Judith and Mary conveyed Mr. Sharp's orders.

"And, as you seem to be struggling to remember much of anything," Mary said, "Judith has agreed to help with your duties until you have regained your confidence."

Judith whipped her head around to Mary.

"I would be very grateful for that, Miss Jardine," Mr. Carlisle said. He looked at Judith, who hadn't yet managed to regain her composure, and frowned. "If it isn't too much to ask, I mean."

"Not at all!" Mary said brightly. "She *did* come visit for the sole purpose of being helpful to me, after all. And helping you is helping me." She turned her sweet, speaking smile on Judith, who returned her own false smile. She might have expected Mary would do something like this.

Mary turned back to Mr. Carlisle. "But for now, you must rest."

"Indeed," Judith cut in. "For the more you rest now, the sooner shall you be able to return to your duties."

"Yes," Mary said. "And in view of that goal, Judith kindly offered to make some of her delightful chicken soup. She can bring that to you when it is ready, then change out Mr. Sharp's bandages once you have eaten."

Judith rubbed her tongue roughly along her teeth, sending Mary a look full of promised revenge, then left the room to make the soup.

❧

JUDITH CARRIED THE TRAY DOWN THE CORRIDOR, stopping just before the door to her bedroom, where she balanced it carefully on one hand and knocked on the door. It grated her pride to be forced into serving Mr. Carlisle in such a way. Even if the reward for all this was humility for Mr. Carlisle, the cost to Judith was proving to be very high as well.

"Come in," Mr. Carlisle said, and Judith pushed the door open and entered.

His overlarge shirt was buttoned at the throat, but because of its size—Mary's husband was shaped more like a pumpkin than a green bean, after all—it gaped open, providing a view of the bandages Mr. Sharp had placed on Mr. Carlisle's wounds. Despite drowning in someone else's shabby clothing, Mr. Carlisle managed to look as handsome as ever, and the fact did nothing to endear him to Judith.

As she set the tray on his lap, he eyed the bowl of soup with a hint of wariness that set up Judith's hackles, reminding her of the expression of distaste he had worn at the dinner party. He would have been well-served if she chose to spill the soup all over him again, but she refrained.

"*Bon appétit*, James," she said ironically, and made her way from the room.

But Mary was waiting just outside the door, and she raised a brow and shook her head as Judith emerged. "Mr. Sharp said he is not to be left alone for long periods of time. He was already alone the entire time you were making the soup."

"If you were so concerned, you could have sat with him then, and you are welcome to do so now."

Mary heaved a great, if somewhat dramatic, sigh and put a hand on her belly. "I am feeling quite done up, I'm afraid."

Judith pinched her lips together, staring her sister down, then gave a little huff and turned back into the room.

Mr. Carlisle paused with the spoon in midair, looking surprised.

"My sister was so kind as to remind me that you are in need of a nursemaid at your side at all times." Judith sat in the rickety chair in the corner of the room, folding her arms across her chest.

"Am I?" Mr. Carlisle asked, eating a heaping spoonful of the soup.

Judith didn't respond.

"This soup is . . . delicious. Do I know how to make it?"

The corner of Judith's mouth quivered, but she

controlled it immediately. "No. I am afraid your cooking skills leave much to be desired." She could safely assume as much.

"Oh. How disappointing. Perhaps you could teach me?"

She glanced at him. The thought of instructing Mr. Carlisle on how to pluck a chicken and cook it was as laughable as it was enticing. And if he had resisted the idea rather than suggesting it, Judith would have been inclined to press the issue. But he had not. How was it possible for someone who had looked at her with so much disgust last week to look at her now with such imploring— and for such a purpose?

"Perhaps," she said evasively. The opportunity would never present itself.

Mr. Carlisle set down his spoon, watching her. "Miss Jardine, I understand that it must put you out a great deal to be obliged to attend to duties that normally fall to me. I sincerely apologize for the trouble I have caused you."

Judith met his gaze. Oh, the trouble he had caused her. She could almost imagine he was apologizing for thrusting a nickname upon her. Either way, she couldn't help but relent toward him at such a frank apology. Had his head injury jolted some kindness into him?

She knew a moment of misgiving as she looked in his eyes. What was she to do with a kind Mr. Carlisle? It had been easy to despise him when he had been rude and neglectful. But what now?

Perhaps he would become more pompous as his

memories returned. Judith had an inkling that that might be for the best. After all, how would the *ton* resist a man who was possessed of kindness, handsome looks, *and* a large fortune?

Thankfully, Judith was not of the *ton*.

"I am not upset with you for being injured," she said. "Forgive me if I have seemed so to you. Are you finished with your soup?"

He hesitated then nodded, and she stood to take the bowl, which was empty.

She picked up the tray, then stopped, looking at Mr. Carlisle. "Would you care for more?"

He gave something between a smile and grimace, then nodded.

She couldn't stop a smile at his sheepish demeanor— nor could she deny the little bit of pleasure she felt knowing he had enjoyed the soup she had made. "There is plenty. I shall bring another bowl."

She fetched another helping as well as two of the rolls that sat nearby, consoling herself with the knowledge that it was in her own best interests and not due to a desire for Mr. Carlisle's approval that she did so. The sooner he regained his strength, the sooner he would regain his memories. That was all.

Judith left Mr. Carlisle to the second bowl of soup and rolls while she prepared a salve and ripped up an old shift of Mary's to use for bandages. When she returned, the bowl was empty, and the rolls were gone.

She moved the tray from his lap to make way for the one she had brought in. "My, but you have an appetite."

"Not a novel occurrence, it would seem." He pulled at the loosely hanging front of the shirt he wore.

Judith laughed and sat down beside him. "Come. Mr. Sharp ordered that your dressings be changed."

"Miss Jardine," Mr. Carlisle said in an apologetic voice, "surely it does not fall to you to do such a thing."

"Oh?" she asked politely. "To whom, then?"

He grimaced but offered no response.

"Now, show me these infamous battle wounds." She tried to keep her voice light and a smile on her face.

He frowned, then gave a little resigned sigh and pulled down the straps of his suspenders.

Judith's heart stopped, and she instinctively looked away.

Mr. Carlisle didn't miss her reaction, and he stopped with his hands on the hem of his shirt, ready to pull it over his head. He let it go and shook his head. "We can leave the dressings till morning. Perhaps then Mr."—he fumbled a bit—"Burns can come assist me."

Judith raised a brow. "Mr. Barry, you mean?"

"That is what I said."

She laughed. "You decidedly did not. You said Mr. Burns. And, no. We will not leave the dressings on until tomorrow. Mr. Sharp would have my head. I am not squeamish." She gave a nod. "Hurry, then."

He wavered a moment, then pulled the shirt over his head, wincing. Two bandages were wrapped around his midsection. Judith focused her attention on the fibers of linen that hung from the strips, though even without allowing her eyes to explore anything else, she had no difficulty recognizing that Mr. Carlisle added athleticism to his accomplishments. A pugilist, no doubt.

The wounds were, thankfully, located on his side and back, which meant Judith needn't look him in the eye at all while she dressed the wounds. It did not, however, save her from a more intimate knowledge than she ever wished for of Mr. Carlisle's powerful build and warm skin. He prevented too much of her focus from resting on such thoughts by asking her questions about his duties and situation, all of which she answered as vaguely as possible, with guilt in her heart and heat in her cheeks.

"Miss Jardine," he said after putting his shirt back on.

"Hmm?" She gathered the old dressings to be washed.

There was a pause. "Am I married?"

She stilled, then slowly set the last dressing on the tray, wondering what had brought about such a question. "You are not."

"Oh."

She looked at him, wondering if he was disappointed or relieved.

He sent her a smile. "Thank you. For everything. I assure you I mean to be back to my duties in the morning."

She shook her head, but he talked over her. "I will not let you take on all my tasks, Miss Jardine. I can see to them."

"Some of them, perhaps. We can speak of that in the

morning, though. For now, what you need is rest, both body and mind." She would much rather he laze about and find excuses not to perform his duties. She would feel less guilty then.

He looked as though he might resist but only nodded.

When Judith had closed the door behind her, she realized that, with Mr. Carlisle in her own bed, she was left without a place to sleep.

She stood in the corridor, brows knit together, eyes on the narrow door in the dark corner at the end. If Mr. Carlisle was to fill the role of servant for a time, he should sleep in the closet—a cramped room with barely enough space for a straw mattress, a wash basin, and a small set of drawers with a tallow candle sitting upon it. It had been Jane's room.

But Judith hadn't the heart to ask him to move there. He was undoubtedly used to sleeping in fairly luxurious circumstances. Judith's bed would be change enough while still allowing him to sleep comfortably enough to aid in his recovery. If he slept well, his memories would hopefully return with the morning, and she could take her room back up again when he left.

The sooner he left, the better. For everyone.

CHAPTER SEVEN

Between the straw poking her every time she moved and the number of times she had hit her head on the low ceiling, Judith did not sleep well. The lack of a fire in the grate when she woke to a chillier morning than usual did nothing to improve her humor. Mary, on the other hand, was in an irritatingly joyful mood, seeming to take no heed of Judith's predicament. All responsibility for Mr. Carlisle she insisted—very unapologetically—upon placing on Judith's shoulders.

"We need more fish," Mary said as she sipped the tea Judith had prepared. "And potatoes, too."

Judith stared at her, soot from her encounter with preparing breakfast and cleaning the hearth smeared across her dress. "And I am to acquire them?"

Mary rubbed her belly and gave a shrug. "Send Mr. Carlisle to the market. *That* is sure to refresh his memory."

"Perhaps I will," Judith set her teacup down with a

clank, then rose from the wicker chair and strode purposefully toward her bedroom.

She pushed the door open and halted.

Mr. Carlisle lay asleep upon the bed. The bedcovers
were in a tangle around him. Had he slept badly as well?
The bandage around his head had shifted so that it was
slung at a diagonal, covering one eye completely and
pushing up his dark hair above the other eye. It was
amusing—and aggravatingly endearing.

She couldn't possibly send him to the market. She
sighed and went back out again.

❀

WHATEVER KINDNESS HAD MOTIVATED JUDITH'S
decision to make the trip to the market herself, it had been
long since expended by the time she reached the cottage
with a basket on one arm and a bursting sack of potatoes
and vegetables hanging from the other.

Mr. Carlisle sat at the table in the sitting room,
drinking a cup of tea at his leisure and laughing at something Mary had just said as she bounced Charlie on her
knee. The bandage had been repositioned on Mr.
Carlisle's head, so that gone was the endearing appearance
that had inspired Judith's act of selflessness.

"You look to be feeling well, James," Judith said in a
brittle, sunny voice. "Have your memories returned?"

His smile faltered slightly. "No. I am afraid not." He
rose from his seat and put out a hand to take the sack

hanging from her arm. If she had not just spent the last two hours squeezing through a crowded market, trying to make her voice heard over those of other aggressive market-goers, and having her feet trod on, his chivalry might have had greater effect.

"Well," Judith said, "Mr. Sharp encouraged us to give you some light work that might help refresh your memories, and I have just the thing." She plopped the basket down on the table, full to bursting with fish. Having Mr. Carlisle clean twenty sardines would even the scales and, she trusted, be sufficiently revolting to spur some memories.

Mr. Carlisle looked at the fish then up at her, bafflement in his eyes.

She smiled at him, ignoring Mary's pointed look. "I shouldn't think that you are yet well enough to see to beating rugs and some of the more physical tasks you are accustomed to, but preparing the fish—*sardines* today—will not require too much of you."

Little Charlie pulled a face as he peered at the basket.

"Nonsense, my love," Judith said as she pinched the toddler's cheek. "A veritable bundle of deliciousness."

"They needn't be prepared beyond cutting off the heads," Mary said. "We can roast them whole."

Judith waved aside her sister's comment, unwilling to settle for so painless a task. "I cannot abide finding bones in my fish. They must certainly be prepared properly."

"Indeed," Mary said with faux interest. She turned to

Mr. Carlisle. "And tell me, James. Do you remember how to prepare fish?"

Mr. Carlisle was still staring at the heap in the basket, where round, glassy eyes stared up at all of them blankly. He blinked and looked up, shaking his head. "I cannot say that I do."

"I suspected as much," Mary said. She looked at Judith with such innocence in her eyes that Judith's smile flickered as she realized what was to come. "Judith will gladly help to refresh your memory. And you, sir"—she faced Charlie toward her, though her belly kept him at a greater distance than usual—"are in need of a washing."

"I can see to that," Judith said eagerly, reaching for Charlie. "After all, you have much more practice cleaning fish than I, Mary. Come, Charlie."

But Mary shifted away from Judith, keeping Charlie from her reach. "All the more reason for you to see to the task. For how will you improve your skill but by practice?" She stood and, taking Charlie by the hand, shot Judith a look that made her want to wring Mary's neck.

Judith took in a deep breath. She had cleaned fish the last time she had come to Portsbury, and she had never wished to repeat the experience. Perhaps it would be worth the pain, though, to see Mr. Carlisle engaged in such an activity.

She retrieved two knives from the kitchen and sat in the chair Mary had occupied, preparing herself for the unsavory task before her.

"Perhaps it will come back to me once I"—Mr. Carlisle

swallowed and picked up one of the fish—"have one in hand."

Only with difficulty did Judith control the impulse to laugh at the utter disgust on Mr. Carlisle's face. He shuddered slightly, and juice from the fish dripped onto his trousers. She watched him for any indication that the scenario might feel in the least bit familiar, but there was none. Was his memory truly gone? Or had his encounter with her at the Brighton ball been so inconsequential that he would never think on it again?

Mr. Carlisle took in a fortifying breath and picked up the knife Judith had set on the table beside him. He set it to the fish with hesitation, then looked at her.

She raised a brow.

"It is not coming back," he said, with enough guilt to soften her slightly.

"No." She rose from the chair and pulled it next to his. "I can see that from the way you are holding it. It is dead, James. You needn't treat it as though you intended to give it a name—"

"Mr. Higgins," he said without any hesitation.

She pinched her lips together to stop their unruliness. "—and a place to sleep."

He flashed her a sidelong glance with eyes full of teasing, and it brought her heart up into her throat.

Well, *that* wouldn't do. She reached for a fish, forcing herself to focus on the distasteful feel of it on her fingers rather than Mr. Carlisle's smile. It worked to great effect, and she suppressed her own shudder as she set it on the small wood platter and straightened her shoulders. "You must hold your knife like this—a light hold is paramount, for otherwise, you risk slipping and cutting yourself, and forgive me, James, but I have no desire for you to add such an injury to the ones you have already acquired. Nor do I not intend to go to the market in your place next week because you are recovering from another accident."

"A light hold," he repeated, letting the knife rest on his hand as he bounced his wrist lightly up and down.

Judith recoiled, and he stopped.

"A light hold, James. Not *no* hold at all."

He smiled, but adjusted his grip accordingly.

"Now," she said, "first, we must get rid of the head."

Mr. Carlisle looked down at the sardine before him. "It is staring at me. Mr. Higgins is staring at me."

"He is not." She pinched her lips together. "*It* is not."

He gave her a challenging glance, indicating the fish before her, and she looked down at it. Its large eye gaped at her, daring her to follow through with her threat.

"Are you scared of a dead fish, James?"

His brow and mouth frowned deeply, and he shook his head decidedly, but as he looked back down at the sardine, the head-shaking slowed and turned into nodding.

Judith couldn't stifle a laugh. "Oh, for heaven's sake! All you need to do is *this*." She steeled herself and made the necessary cut with her knife, then she turned the fish over and repeated the exercise.

By the time she had shown Mr. Carlisle how to finish the task, her stomach was churning. "I will go retrieve the salt to preserve what we will not be using," she said in an unstable voice.

She hurried up from her seat and toward the small larder at the far side of the kitchen, opening the window that looked toward the sea and breathing the fresh air deeply. When she returned with the salt, Mr. Carlisle looked up at her with culpability in his gaze.

She looked at the table and brought a hand up to cover her mouth, which trembled traitorously. "Good heavens! What have you done to poor Mr. Higgins?" His sardine was, indeed, headless, but the rest was . . . well, mutilated.

Mr. Carlisle grimaced apologetically, his face looking a bit green, and Judith's mirth escaped in the form of a small snort

His brows shot up at the unladylike sound.

Clearing her throat, she sat down beside him again and set down the salt, taking a new sardine from the basket.

"I shall do better next time," he promised, taking up another fish. "I am determined to learn." He set the knife to it.

"Stop," Judith cried with a hand up, moving her chair even closer to him. "No wonder you are struggling. You are still not holding the knife correctly. It should be held like *this*." She fixed his grasp on the knife and guided him in the cutting process, forcing herself again to focus on the gruesome details of the task rather than her hand on his. There was *nothing* romantic about cutting a fish with a man, whatever her heart might say.

The next hour was one of the strangest Judith had ever passed, full of fish bits, laughter, and frustration as Mr. Carlisle showed no aptitude at all for the task at hand. The salt rested on the table, unused as yet, and only three sardines remained in the basket.

"I think we shall have to content ourselves with picking out the bones for dinner this evening," Judith said resignedly.

Mr. Carlisle was looking sickly after a particularly unfortunate attempt at cutting a sardine, but he nodded. Judith looked at the results of her unsuccessful foray into teaching, and her own stomach swam at the sight. It—and the smell that permeated the air—were overwhelming.

"A fish massacre," Mr. Carlisle said with obvious frustration.

"A one-man fish massacre, no less," Judith replied, looking away from the macabre sight.

"Perhaps you could cut the last ones, and I can simply watch."

She sighed and placed the three sardines on the table, cutting them in turn, her thoughts and feelings conflicting. She had managed to make Mr. Carlisle look green, but the task had not elicited any of his memories as she had anticipated it might, and, worse by far, the more time she spent with him, the more she was coming to like him.

"There," she said. "See how easy that was?" She looked up at him and stilled. His gaze was on her, and a little hint of a smile pulled up at the corner of his mouth. But it was not that which kept her attention. It was the fish bits that had somehow made their way to the bandage on his head—including an eye.

She fought valiantly to control herself, but it was a lost cause, and it was through eyes leaking with tears of laughter that she attempted to explain to Mr. Carlisle the object of her mirth. Through her pointing and unintelligible speech, he managed to gather that his bandage was the culprit, and he lifted it from his head, turning it in his hands with a look of disgust on his face until he found the spark to Judith's amusement.

He gave a start and threw the bandage, which landed on Judith's lap. Her mouth dropped open, and she immediately picked it up with two fingers and tossed it back.

Mr. Carlisle was smiling now, and he held it up threateningly. Judith reached her hands for the mess of fish on the table and gave him a look of warning. He swiftly dropped the bandage on his lap and put both hands up in surrender.

"Good choice," Judith said, smiling at the genuine dismay in his eyes. "And now, I think it is time both of us cleaned up."

There was a hint of reluctance in the way he agreed. Judith felt it, too, and it struck a chord of fear within her.

A man who could make her feel loath to leave the cleaning of fish was a dangerous man indeed.

CHAPTER EIGHT

James helped Miss Jardine clean up his embarrassing efforts at preparing fish. Not only had he no memory of ever executing such a task, he had also obviously lost the skill for it. Beyond that, more than once, he had come perilously near to losing the tea he had drunk just beforehand.

How had he managed to do such a task when the sight and smell of the dead fish made his stomach turn? Had he simply suffered through it for years? Or was the aversion something he had acquired with the accident?

The truth was, nothing about life here felt familiar—nothing felt right. Nothing except Miss Jardine. And that in itself was wrong, wasn't it? In his capacity as a servant, there was no place for the attraction and admiration James had been feeling.

"That will do for now," Miss Jardine said as she

removed her apron and motioned for him to follow her down the corridor.

They reached the bedchamber he had been occupying, and Miss Jardine entered, taking a few garments from the armoire in the corner. James frowned as she gave him a polite smile and exited.

"I shall fetch you some fresh clothing," she said. "And once I have changed, I shall bring more strips and the salve I made yesterday."

James nodded, but he was confused. Was this Miss Jardine's room? He had never thought on the subject long enough to wonder. He hadn't recognized the room as his own, but he hadn't recognized *anything*.

When Miss Jardine returned a few minutes later with folded clothing in hand, he took it from her. "Miss Jardine?"

She paused at the door.

"Is this your bedchamber?" he asked.

She took a moment before responding. "Yes."

"Then where are you sleeping?"

A pause. "In one of the other rooms."

"But why put me here, if there are other rooms I might be in? There is no need to inconvenience you."

Miss Jardine looked uncomfortable with the line of questioning. "I thought you could do with a bit of space."

He frowned more deeply still, and the gesture tugged lightly at the wound on the back of his head. "My normal bedchamber lacks space, then?"

Her lips pursed together. "Yes. Yes, it does."

"Miss Jardine," he said. "I have put you out quite enough. And I assure you, I have no need of extra space. I would prefer it if you returned here and I to my own bedchamber."

A flicker of humor danced in her eyes. "Would you really?"

Her strange answer gave him pause, but he nodded.

"Follow me, then," she said.

He did as instructed, and they emerged into the dim corridor, where the smell of dampness was strong. Miss Jardine walked to a small, uneven door at the end of the corridor and put out a hand in a showy gesture. There was an amused smile on her face, and James's eyes lingered on her for a moment before returning to the door.

The door stuck as he tried to open it, but with a more forceful tug, it gave way. It was dark within, and it took a moment for his eyes to make anything out. As they did, his eyebrows went up, and he could feel Miss Jardine's gaze on him.

It was no bedchamber—or not a proper one, at least. There was a small, lumpy bed and a washstand with two drawers, both of which looked to be broken. It lacked a window, so the only light which reached the space was the trifling bit that existed in the corridor.

"This is where you slept last night?" James asked.

"Yes." She tilted her head to the side. "Well, *sleep* is a generous term. Let us say rather that this is where I spent the night."

James glanced at the woman beside him, who looked

at him with wrinkles of amusement beside her eyes. It was hard for him to comprehend how she could fit in such a space, to say nothing of his own, taller form. And he was not now anywhere near as large as he had once been, based on the clothing that belonged to him. Just the thought of attempting to fit within made his legs cry out in protest.

"Return to the other bedchamber, James," Miss Jardine said with an understanding smile.

He shook his head, staring again at the mattress. The fabric was threadbare in many places, with straw poking through.

"That is an order," Miss Jardine said. "And might I also suggest that you take advantage of your time there? For I doubt I shall be feeling so generous tomorrow."

James hesitated, wanting to resist her order but laboring under the force of the knowledge that he had no right to nay say her. He was a servant.

Before he could decide what to do, Miss Jardine was slipping into the small space, hunched over in a way that, in spite of himself, brought a smile to James's face.

"Excuse me," she said as she closed the door. It refused to shut all the way, and there were sounds of struggle.

James gave the door a push, and it slammed into place.

"Thank you," came her muffled voice.

James stared at the door another moment, then sighed and went back to his temporary bedchamber to change his clothing.

His injuries felt less painful and tight than they had

the day before, but it was largely owing to the generous size of both the old and new garments that he was able to change them with so little trouble.

Ten minutes later, he sat on the edge of the bed with no sign of Miss Jardine. It must be difficult, indeed, to do anything in the small space she had been in, to say nothing of changing clothing. He had little doubt she would air her grievances on the subject to him. She was a strange woman—hot and cold by turns.

She was likely occupied with helping care for her nephew. He could hear the ear-splitting sounds of Charlie's displeasure being made known.

Presently, there was a knock on his door, and he shot to his feet. His head throbbed at the overzealous action, and he shut his eyes, taking in a deep breath. He shouldn't be so eager for her company.

He opened the door and blinked. Mr. Sharp stood before him, spectacles perched halfway down his nose. His leather bag was slung over his shoulder, a copy of a newspaper sticking out.

"Mr. Sharp," James said, trying to infuse his voice with pleasantness instead of disappointment. "Come in."

Mr. Sharp was not one for exchanging civilities, and he set right to the task of asking questions and examining James's wounds.

"These should be bandaged," he said, displeasure evident in his voice. "I gave precise orders on the subject."

"I was just waiting for Miss Jardine to come with fresh ones when you arrived."

He gave a grunt and opened his bag.

"Mr. Sharp?"

Another grunt.

"None of my memories have yet returned. Do you anticipate they will?"

"I believe so."

The curt answer was hardly invitation to continue, but James couldn't help himself. "I just find it so strange how unfamiliar everything continues to be."

Mr. Sharp offered no response, only continuing his inspection of James's head.

"May I give you an example?"

Receiving no refusal, he proceeded. "Just today, I attempted one of my regular duties—cleaning out and preparing fish. One would think that doing something which should be so familiar to me would have roused some sliver of a memory at least, no?"

A small grunt.

"But it did not. And not only that, sir, but I was hard-pressed not to retch with the sight and smell of the fish. And furthermore, even with Miss Jardine's aid, I could not manage to carry out the task properly even *once*." He shook his head, troubled again at the memory.

Mr. Sharp moved to the injuries on James's side and back, moving his bag of instruments to the floor so he could sit down. "Blows to the head can be life-altering. I have seen them change people in very strange ways. Your speech, for instance."

"What do you mean?"

The surgeon chuckled. "I have never met a servant with such proper speech." He shrugged. "It wouldn't be the strangest result of a head injury I have ever heard of."

James didn't respond. He might have asked Mr. Sharp a hundred more questions, but the man's answers only led to even more questions. Would James never remember life before the accident?

Mr. Sharp stood and reached for his bag, eyes on James's head. "Whatever Miss Jardine put on the wounds, it seems to have worked well. The injury on your head should remain bandaged tonight, but you may remove it tomorrow if you are feeling well enough." He began to move toward the door, then turned. "As for your memories, don't despair just yet. Sometimes, it only takes something insignificant. It is merely a matter of finding that spark. Good day."

James sat on the edge of the bed for a moment, pondering on the surgeon's visit. The sound of Charlie's cries had dissipated, yet there was still no sign of Miss Jardine.

He stepped into the corridor, intending to go to the kitchen, where he could hear the clamor of preparation occurring. But he stopped short, listening.

No, he wasn't imagining it. He hurried to the door at the end of the corridor and yanked it open.

Miss Jardine fell forward, and he caught her under the arms. She smelled of straw and violets—a strange combination—and she hurried to push herself to a stand, using James as a bolster.

Her eyes sparkled, and she brushed roughly at her skirts with a huff. "Is *everyone* in this house deaf?"

James's eyebrows shot up, and his mouth trembled with laughter. He covered it with a hand, well-aware of how unwelcome his reaction would be. "Were you in there that entire time?"

"Do you find that amusing?" she asked.

He pulled his lips between his teeth, shaking his head and hoping his own eyes didn't betray him by laughing the way Miss Jardine's sometimes did.

"I suppose you expect my thanks for releasing me"— she kicked at the door, which hit the frame at its odd angle and rebounded, forcing her to hasten to the side—"but as you were the one who entrapped me in the first place, you will, I am afraid, have to do without."

"Entrapped you?" he asked. "I thought *I* was the one with the faulty memory! Perhaps you will recall that I expressed my desire that you should return to your own bedchamber."

"And then promptly cemented me into the closet." She gave another huff. "You may sleep in my bedchamber tonight, James, but tomorrow, you will have the doubtful pleasure of occupying this space again." She strode toward the kitchen, leaving him in the corridor.

He smiled as he watched her disappear, but she returned quickly with the salve and strips of fabric. He followed her into the bedchamber and sat down upon the bed, watching Miss Jardine's fiery movements with wariness. "Perhaps we should wait until . . ."

She raised her brows challengingly. "Until?"

"Until your desire to harm me has subsided a bit?"

"I can quite easily separate my feelings for you from my actions, James." She tore a piece of fabric to make it smaller, and his eyes widened.

But she proved to be correct. So correct, in fact, that James almost wished otherwise. Her light touch on his wounds, the soft hand she used to stabilize herself on his skin—it did nothing to help James toward his goal of smothering his attraction to her. Was the draw he felt to her new, or had he felt it before his injury, too?

Thankfully—*and* regrettably, somehow—she made quick and silent work of it. There was no trace of anger left in her eyes afterward. In fact, James could have sworn they were troubled. But it was not his place to pursue such a subject.

"Tomorrow morning, I will resume my duties," he said.

Her lips pinched together in dissatisfaction, though why, he couldn't tell.

"You object?" he asked.

"I do if you perform them like you performed your duty today."

He let out a rueful laugh. "Your patience for teaching me is understandably spent."

She looked at him, silent for a moment. "I will *try* to teach you. And I trust you will be rested enough after another night in this luxurious bed to enable your most exemplary work."

"I would gladly take my rightful place in the closet," he pointed out.

Those intent eyes fixed on him again, searching his face. "No. I gave you an order, James. I trust I will not be obliged to repeat myself again." She gave him a haughty look—the type that was entirely undermined by her insistence upon taking the cramped closet for herself.

However little James remembered of life before he had woken in Miss Jardine's bed, he was grateful that he *had* woken to find himself employed in the home of women as likable as Mrs. Bradford and Miss Jardine. What if he had woken to find himself the servant of a man like Mr. Sharp? He hoped Mr. Bradford would be as amiable as his wife and sister-in-law, whenever he returned.

With the help of both women, James learned how to prepare potatoes and sardines—or what was left of them, anyway—for dinner. And though he did resist when Mrs. Bradford insisted that he join them for dinner, his protestations were easily overcome. "You have oft sat down to dine with us in the past," she had said. And when he entered Miss Jardine's bedchamber to settle in for the night, it was with a strange sense of contentment.

He reached to pull off one of his boots, and his hand brushed something at the base of the bed. It was a newspaper, and he picked it up with curiosity. It must have fallen out of Mr. Sharp's bag earlier.

The first page was covered in fine print, lists of advertisements for servants. James read through a few of them, wondering if he himself had answered just such a notice.

There were so many questions about his past. How had he learned to read, for instance? Did he have family still living? How old was he? Why was he not married?

As for the last question, a part of him wondered if the attraction he felt for Miss Jardine was one of the few things connecting him to his past. There was something that felt so familiar about her. Had he felt before as he did now, always wishing to spend more time near her?

He sighed and opened the newspaper, letting his eyes run over the next page—two notices of impending marriages, a number of paragraphs devoted to bills coming up for debate when Parliament resumed and—he frowned at a paragraph in the center of the page.

"Information sought regarding the whereabouts of Mr. James Carlisle, son and heir of Mr. Henry Carlisle and Mrs. Margaret Carlisle of Lower Birchmouth, who was last seen in Brighton on the twelfth of June. A reward of five pounds is offered to anyone in possession of reliable intelligence on the subject, to be presented at . . ."

James's mind whirled, and he stared at the name: James Carlisle.

And with such a spark, the flicker of memory fanned into a small flame.

CHAPTER NINE

J udith turned over sleepily in bed, only for her head and arm to hit against the wall. She groaned softly and rubbed the spot on her forehead with a hand.

Thunk thunk. The sound forced a greater awareness onto her.

Who in the world could be knocking on her door in the middle of the night? Her eyes flew open. Perhaps it was Mary and the baby was on its way.

She stood, careful not to let her head hit the steeply sloped ceiling, and slipped on her wrapper before opening the door hurriedly.

Mr. Carlisle stood before her with the sort of smile on his face that, to be quite frank, was unsuitable for such a time of night.

"What is it?" she asked, brushing aside both her irritation and the vain worry she felt over her appearance.

He hesitated a bit. "You said to wake you when the cock crowed, did you not?"

Was it truly morning already? She had spent a great deal of time the night before berating herself for ever having offered up her own bedchamber to Mr. Carlisle. So far, very little about her desire to teach him a lesson had gone according to plan, and she owed at least a portion of that to her own pesky—and oft-regretted—moments of charity toward him. She was finding it difficult not to like Mr. Carlisle—and to like him more than she cared to admit.

When she emerged a few minutes later, dressed for the day, he was leaning against the wall, humming softly, and she knew a bit of anticipation at the prospect of spending the day with him.

"Is it not cold in that closet during the winter months?" he asked quietly as they passed the door to Mary and Charlie's room.

"Yes," she said. "That is when you sleep by the fire in the sitting room." Or, at least, that was what Jane had done.

He looked over at her, his dark eyebrows raised.

She felt an annoying need to defend her sister's circumstances. "If Mary's husband manages to be offered the position he is seeking, their lodgings would be much improved."

"Would you go with them? With us?"

She shook her head. "I am only here to help during my sister's confinement."

"But you have visited on other occasions? While I have been employed here?"

She glanced at him warily. It was natural for him to have questions, of course, but she disliked having to answer them—to perjure herself.

"I only ask," he said, "because very few things have struck a chord in my memory as of yet. But you . . ." He looked at her thoughtfully, searchingly, and her blood flowed warmer. "There is something familiar about you."

Her heart pattered more quickly, and she knew a certain dismay at the thought that he might recognize her and discover the truth. That would mean the end of things, and while she had been wishing for that precise thing since Mr. Sharp had forbidden her from oversetting Mr. Carlisle, she found that just now, she wasn't quite ready for it. It must be due to the simple fact that she enjoyed being in a position of superiority. Her entire life, her family had lingered on the fringes of polite society, looked down upon by people like Mr. Carlisle. Of course, she would find some enjoyment in the tables being turned.

There was nothing else to her feelings. She wouldn't let there be.

She changed the subject. "You have removed the bandage on your head." It was unfortunate, really. It had been easier to forget how handsome he was with it covering part of his face and pushing his hair up at awkward angles.

"It still smells of fish."

She laughed as they came to the hearth. "Then I am

glad you have removed it. I have no desire to be smelling you all day." She turned to the hearth. "Now, the first task is to light the fire." She took the flint box from the mantel and handed it to him.

He stared down at it, then up at her, a blank look in his eyes.

Judith let out a dramatic, resigned sigh and took the box back. "What would you do without me? You cannot remember even the most basic of tasks." She crouched down, and he followed suit.

"*Or* perhaps I am simply finding excuses for your company."

Judith whipped her head around to look at him. He was teasing her—it was written in his laughing eyes as clear as the stars in the sky, and it nettled her.

"In misplacing your memory," she said severely, "you seem to have misplaced your sense of propriety as well."

"Did I have one before the accident?" he asked.

Judith's mind flashed back to the way he had ignored her almost entirely at dinner. "Not much, no."

"Then what has induced your sister to keep me on as a servant?"

Judith drove the striker along the flint so that Mr. Carlisle could see. She handed it to him. "She hasn't the heart to send you back to the life you had before."

"The life I had before . . ." Mr. Carlisle said, watching her. "What was it like?"

She chose not to respond directly to the question.

"Despite your episodes of impudence, you are much improved since working here."

"Am I?" The words themselves were harmless enough, but they were said with a dose of teasing—one might have even said *flirtation*—that affected her far more than was fair.

"You mustn't sound so puffed up about it," she said. "Transforming a pig into an ass may be an improvement, but both beasts leave much to be desired."

Mr. Carlisle let out a laugh and attempted to emit a spark with the striker and flint. He failed, and Judith was obliged to guide him. He showed no indication of ever having performed the duty required of him, and little wonder. It was very possible he had never had to light a fire in his life.

And while Judith was quick to express her frustration with his ineptitude, Mr. Carlisle was just as quick to make her laugh, and she found that the normally tedious tasks of cleaning the stove and the carpets were much less so with him for company.

The latter activity was the first he showed any natural aptitude for. They set the rugs, which were full of dirt from the dry summer roads, to hang over the branch of the tree behind Mary's house and, with the fresh sea breeze assisting them, took turns beating them.

Mr. Carlisle clapped at Judith's more forceful attempts, and she accepted the praise with the sort of graceful curtsies she had given the night of the Brighton ball. She pretended to give him instruction, as well, but in truth, he needed none.

Breathless after a dozen turns each, they rested their backs against the crooked trunk of the tree, which offered a view of the sea beyond. The sun-kissed water stretched on for miles, until the horizon became so shrouded in mist, it was impossible to see where the sea ended and the sky began.

"I have a question," Mr. Carlisle announced. "Does it still count as impudence if I warn you of it?" The trunk of the tree was wide, but not so wide that they could both lean against it without standing up against each other.

"Yes, James." She shot him an unamused look. "It does."

He gave a *humph* and crossed his arms.

Judith tried to fight off her curiosity at what he had been about to say. She could feel her feet on dangerous ground, and it wasn't a question of whether the ground would give out, but when.

"Although," Mr. Carlisle said, sending her a sidelong glance, "one cannot expect an ass to act like anything other than an ass . . ."

She tried to control a smile.

He paused a moment, and his expression became more pensive. "You are not married."

She stiffened involuntarily, and her smile disappeared. "A comment fit for an ass, indeed." She stepped away from the tree.

"No, no," Mr. Carlisle said, and he pulled her back by the hand.

Judith's heart leapt into her throat.

"You mistake my meaning," he said, and the teasing in his eyes was gone. "I was only wondering if there was a particular reason for the fact."

"Must there be a reason?" She cocked an eyebrow at the hand he still held, and he dropped it. The regret she felt when he did bothered her deeply.

He shrugged. "I lost my memories, Miss Jardine, not my senses, and it stands to reason that a woman with as much to recommend her as you has had opportunity to marry."

She gave a little snort, and he frowned.

"What? Why do you scoff?"

Judith didn't respond immediately. How could she explain that she might have received an offer of marriage if it weren't for him? He had no memory of their encounter. Perhaps, though, when his memories returned, he would remember what she said now and her words would encourage him to act with less arrogance toward other women in positions like Judith's.

"Impudence is still impudence when it is couched in flattery, James." She stared at the waves rolling in toward the shore. "In any case, you betray your lack of understanding when you say such things. I live in a world in between—too humble to deserve the notice of those above me in station, but just lofty enough not to be noticed by those below me in station."

"Well, there, you're wrong, Miss Jardine."

She looked at him.

"You were the first thing *I* noticed when I woke," he said.

She gave another scoff. "You could hardly have noticed anything else. I placed myself directly in your line of vision."

"But I haven't stopped noticing you since."

She swallowed, all too aware of her heart thundering. If a week ago, she had been told she would hear such words on the lips of Mr. Carlisle—the man who had taken no notice of her at all—it would have been with the anticipation of feeling undeniable pride and a sense of victory. But that was not what she felt now. She felt hope. And she felt as though, of all things, she might cry. Both things terrified her.

In any case, a servant should be slapped and dismissed for such presumption.

But Mr. Carlisle was not her servant, nor was he her sister's servant. He was *no one's* servant at all.

"I think these rugs have been sufficiently beaten," she said. "And we have much left to accomplish."

The best thing would be to ignore his flirtation and make it clear to Mr. Carlisle—and herself—that her role was that of mistress instructing a new servant, because less and less about their interactions felt like those of servant and mistress.

CHAPTER TEN

James paused at the door, watching Miss Jardine inside her sister's room as she aired out the sheets. The afternoon light poured through the open window, illuminating her from behind. She was humming lightly as she saw to her work, and James felt a little ache in his chest at the idyllic image. Even with the return of his memories, what it was that was so familiar about her still eluded him.

He had begun the day with several objectives in mind. Firstly, he wished to postpone his return to normal life, as that would entail facing the expected visit to Miss Garrett, and he was not at all certain how he intended to approach that meeting. He shuddered every time he pictured her stare fixed upon him, but he also shuddered at the thought of his father's disappointment if he should fail to "come up to scratch." He would use the day to ponder on that dilemma.

Secondly, he had hoped to seek enlightenment—very carefully, albeit—regarding Miss Jardine and Mrs. Bradford's objectives in making him believe he was their servant. A servant, of all things! In his initial anger and bafflement, he had nearly gone to demand an explanation from Miss Jardine last night. But could he count on her telling him the truth? A person who would deceive someone as she had been deceiving James was clearly not to be relied upon.

The entire situation was so incredible as to be lunatic—and yet, simultaneously comical and intriguing. In the end, his curiosity determined his final aim for the day: to turn the tables on Miss Jardine. He had considered other options, of course: berating her, leaving the house without a word—he would have been justified in either. But those options would both be so fleeting and dissatisfying.

No, he would amuse himself much better this way, making Miss Jardine regret the promise she had made to guide him through his so-called *duties*. It seemed only fair, given what she was doing to *him*. And certainly more enjoyable than facing the realities of his life.

But teasing Miss Jardine was proving to be even more entertaining and agreeable than he had foreseen. And as he watched her for another moment, broom in his hand, he made a decision.

Based on the date he had seen on the newspaper Mr. Sharp had left, he had a week until the meeting his father had arranged with Miss Garrett and Lord Linscott. What would happen if he never appeared for it? No one could blame him for being too indisposed to attend such an engagement—he *had* lost his memory, after all. And if he waited long enough, Sir William would offer for Miss Garrett. She would be well taken care of, and James would be liberated from the undesired connection.

He would stay. And he would find out what Miss Jardine was about while he was at it.

❀

MR. SHARP CALLED THE NEXT DAY AND, DESPITE THE niggling guilt in James's stomach, he gave the surgeon no indication that his memory had returned.

"As for injury to body," the man said to James and the two sisters, "he is well on his way to recovery. As regards injury to mind, I cannot deny that I am disappointed. We must begin to consider the possibility that the memories shall not return."

James looked at Miss Jardine, whose eyes were round with . . . was it dismay? The news certainly did not seem welcome, and her reaction perplexed him. If she had been trusting that his memories would return, what in the world was she about? Why not simply tell him the truth?

She knew at the very least he was not her sister's servant—there was no doubt at all about that. But did she know his real identity? He suspected she did, and the fact that he couldn't think *how* they might have become acquainted grated him unbearably. They were not the sort of people he would have had occasion to meet in Society, and he was certain he had never before been to Portsbury. If he had not taken it in his head to go out rowing that fateful morning and subsequently found himself in increasingly rough waters, he never *would* have been to Portsbury.

He was determined to untangle the whole mess.

That determination was certainly tested, though, for life as a servant was anything but easy. His time from dawn till dusk was occupied with chores, and the closet— fiend seize that blasted closet!—was a trial, indeed, to sleep in, if he was fortunate enough to sleep at all. His experience there made him all the more appreciative of Miss Jardine having slept there the first two nights of his stay.

Evenings were the most difficult for James. It was then that he seriously considered ending the baffling charade they were all living, for it was then that he was alone. His time during the day was often spent in the company of Miss Jardine as she oversaw his tasks and instructed him in improving them. He made sure that there was enough progress in the performance of his duties not to raise questions or lead to his termination as a servant—ha!—but little enough progress that Miss Jardine was obliged to assist him from time to time. He took great joy in teasing her and in flirting with her just enough to discomfit her. He enjoyed her company.

Once or twice, he wondered whether the sisters shared a hope of forging a connection between himself and Miss Jardine. This was largely due to Mrs. Bradford's apparent eagerness to throw them into tasks together.

Perhaps they hoped to arrange for a match between the two of them before he could become aware of his true situation in life?

But such a belief was unsustainable. James had heard Miss Jardine plead with her sister on more than one occasion to allow her to take on the care of Charlie in lieu of engaging in a task alongside James. He was baffled—and a little hurt, if he was being honest—by those instances. But Mrs. Bradford was always quick to insist that she wished to keep Charlie to herself so that she might spend as much time with him as possible before the new baby arrived.

Miss Jardine was difficult to puzzle out, in truth. She could be impatient with James—and often was—but this he found easy to forgive. After all, he had made it his goal to make her life more difficult. In addition, her shows of wit pleased him, and it became an ambition of his to make her laugh. He always felt exhilaration and satisfaction when he succeeded.

At other times, though, he knew a desire to do much more than make her laugh. He had caught himself with the impulse to take her in his arms. His wish to tease and torture her had become confusingly mixed up with other developing feelings.

The ease of being with her and the knowledge that she and Mrs. Bradford would struggle to get along without him made the uncomfortable nights more bearable. Every now and then—usually when he had just hit his head on the unforgivably slanted ceiling in the closet—James would fall into a fit of laughter at the absurdity of his current situation.

Just shy of a week after his arrival, James sat on a stump outside the cottage, just under the kitchen window, letting the sea breeze ruffle his hair and cool the sweat on his brow. It was a particularly hot day, and he had nearly finished beating the rugs when he had noticed a stain upon the one from the sitting room—compliments of Charlie having managed to steal a few blackberries undetected.

More and more, Miss Jardine had begun leaving him to perform tasks on his own, only coming to check on the final result of his work. He disliked the development, but he could only pretend incompetence for so long.

Her voice sailed through the open window above him. "And what if his memory never *does* return, Mary?"

James stilled, cocking an ear, though he could easily hear their voices without doing so.

"Then I will happily keep him on as a servant," Mrs. Bradford said.

Miss Jardine let out an impatient noise.

"To be sure," Mrs. Bradford continued, "I had my doubts he could learn how to be a satisfactory one—particularly with the fish-cleaning debacle—but he has improved significantly, you must admit."

"Yes," Miss Jardine said incredulously, "but only after great pains have been taken on my end."

"And I applaud your efforts, Judy. I think members of

the *ton* in general would benefit from knowing what a day in the life of a servant is like."

"Undoubtedly," Miss Jardine replied, "but you cannot seriously mean to keep him on, Mary! To deprive him of his family and his family of him, to say nothing of keeping him from the life he was born into. You must be joking."

"*You* certainly seem not to mind spending time with him." James could hear the smile in Mrs. Bradford's voice, and his heart beat more quickly.

"What in heaven's name are you talking about?"

"Oh, Judy, don't pretend! Not with me. I can see how things lie with you, plain as day."

James leaned closer, cursing the beating of his heart, which had grown so loud in his ears, he feared he might not hear what was said next.

"You are being ridiculous," Miss Jardine said in a clipped voice. "Though that should come as no surprise to me, I suppose. You are hardly subtle in your efforts to throw us together, as though anything could come of that."

"And why not?"

Miss Jardine scoffed. "Enough, Mary. I know you are only amusing yourself, but no more, please. It is time to tell him the truth."

"No, no," Mrs. Bradford said hurriedly. "I am sorry for teasing, Judy. I can see you do not find it funny, which can only mean your feelings run deeper than I had thought. But please do not tell him. Not just yet. When George returns, you have my blessing, but . . ."

"But what?" Miss Jardine sounded exasperated.

"I feel much safer with him here while George is away," Mrs. Bradford said in an apologetic voice. "Only think! What if the baby were to come? My time is drawing near, and I have been feeling pains for a few days now. *You* would be obliged to go fetch someone, and *I* would be in no fit state to care for Charlie."

There was a pause.

"Just a few more days, Judy. That is all I ask. And then you are free to tell him whatever you wish."

There was silence, finally punctuated by a sigh from Miss Jardine.

Footsteps sounded, approaching the door that led to the back of the cottage and out to where James was seated.

He picked up the stick he had been using to beat the rugs and hurried to his feet, rushing over to the branch where a rug was still draped and beginning to hit it. He hoped Miss Jardine didn't realize that the sound had been absent for the past few minutes.

As for what Mrs. Bradford had implied about her sister's feelings for him, he hardly knew what to hope for.

CHAPTER ELEVEN

A s she approached, Judith chose to look at the rippling rug in order to keep her eyes from admiring the man beating it. It was something she had been catching herself doing far too often—admiring Mr. Carlisle—and it frustrated her to no end. When had her disdain for him turned to admiration? And how had she hidden it so ill that Mary had noticed?

Mr. Carlisle turned toward her, wiping a dirty, hanging sleeve across his brow as he met her gaze. A discarded cravat hung from one of the smaller branches, and sweat glistened on the part of his chest visible through the gap in his overlarge shirt. In all her plans to humiliate him, she had never anticipated he would look so utterly charming and unruffled as she did so.

"You might have left this task for this evening when it is cooler," she said.

He shrugged. "There is something rewarding about perspiring after a job well done."

She raised a brow. How would the Mr. Carlisle of two weeks ago feel about hearing such words on his own lips? "A job well done, you say? I think *I* shall be the judge of that." She stepped over to the rug to inspect it. Her lips pinched together. It *did* look well-beaten.

Mary was right. Mr. Carlisle had improved greatly in the past few days. She looked at him, only to find his gaze fixed upon her, watching her carefully. Was he so anxious for her approval?

"An acceptable job," she said begrudgingly.

He inclined his head in a formal gesture. "You overwhelm me, Miss Jardine. Tell me, now. Does this mean I have reached new heights? Am I no longer an ass?"

She was finding it harder and harder to stop her smiles around him. Or perhaps he was getting better and better at eliciting them. "Let us not be premature."

✿

"THIS IS ALL?" JUDITH ASKED IN DISMAY.

Mary's shoulders lifted in a helpless gesture. "The fish you bought were meant to last much longer than two meals, Judy."

They stood in the kitchen together, Charlie tugging on his mother's skirts while the two of them looked at the last of the potatoes and the empty larder.

"But market day isn't for two days," Judith replied.

"I know."

Judith stared at the three potatoes—the smallest ones, which had fallen to the bottom of the sack—and bit her lip.

Mr. Carlisle appeared, holding an empty water basin in the crook of his arm. He smiled at them as he approached but, seeing their expressions, his gait slowed and he frowned.

"Is something the matter?"

Judith looked at Mary, avoiding Mr. Carlisle's eye. It was silly, and she knew it, but she was hesitant to explain the situation to him. Not because it was his fault the sardines hadn't lasted as long as they had been meant to. Her hesitation was because of her pride. What had he said at the dinner? *Good breeding cannot be bought, of course, but it does go hand-in-hand with money.*

Whatever the state of Mr. Carlisle's memory, his prejudices must be lurking beneath the surface. And when he knew that there was no food—and no money for food in the house—what would he be left to infer about Judith and Mary?

But Judith didn't want to care for Mr. Carlisle's opinion. A man who would assume such things didn't deserve that she should allow his opinions to hold any weight.

"We have no food left," she said. It came out sounding more like a challenge than the simple statement of a fact.

His eyebrows went up, and he blinked. "Oh."

Judith felt her pride flare up again at the expression on his face. "I'm afraid that the massacre upended Mary's plans for dinner."

She immediately regretted the words at the look of guilt on Mr. Carlisle's face.

"Of course," he said. "I should have thought of that. I sincerely apologize, and I assure you, I will . . . I will make amends."

Mary shook her head. "You needn't concern yourself with it, James. There is nothing you can do."

"I can fish," he said suddenly. "I will catch them myself."

Judith tilted her head to the side, her worry and pride giving way to amusement. "You think you can fish? Surely, you haven't forgotten what happened last time you attempted that?"

He smiled responsively, though there was still a hint of guilt in his eyes. "I can try." He raised his brows. "Or I could be taught."

Judith scoffed. "I'm afraid our need for food is rather more urgent than the time it would take for you to relearn such a skill."

He shrugged. "I should like to try."

He was serious, and Judith couldn't help but like him the better for it, even if the mere thought of trying to teach him such a skill exhausted her. Had they been so successful in convincing him of his past as a servant that he truly thought he had once possessed such an ability? What would his reaction be to discover that his only accomplishments were dancing cotillions and making bows?

"We *do* have the equipment for it," Mary said.

Judith shot her an annoyed look.

"What?" she said defensively. "We do. It is on the side of the cottage."

"I cannot blame you for having little desire to teach me," Mr. Carlisle said to Judith. "I can make the attempt on my own. Or perhaps there will be a kindly fisherman who will take pity on me."

As he left the room, Mary shot Judith a look that could only be described as that of a chastising mother. "It is not wise for him to go alone, Judy."

"Why must he go at all?" Judith retorted. "No one asked him to."

"We must eat," Mary said significantly. "And it is very kind of him to offer, even if he is unsuccessful. You *did* want him to learn humility, did you not?"

"Yes," Judith said, resignedly reaching for her pelisse. "I did. But if eating is our goal, I should likely have better success fishing on my own."

She hurried to catch up with Mr. Carlisle, who had reached the side of the house and was gathering the fishing equipment together. He glanced up as she approached.

"Have you come to help me or dissuade me?" he asked.

"To protect you," she said, reaching for the bucket. "And ensure that we have something to eat for dinner. You left without even inquiring about a vessel for your expedition."

He smiled mischievously. "I hoped you would follow."

She scoffed and set the bucket down again. "You deserve that I should leave right now."

"Very likely," he said, giving no indication at all that he expected her implied threat to be carried out.

She hesitated another moment, then grabbed the bucket and led the way to the path that would take them to the beach.

Mary and George owned a small boat of somewhat questionable integrity which, when not in use, was kept hidden in the reeds just above the beach. Judith and Mr. Carlisle set their equipment inside it and together pulled it down the grassy slope to the sand below.

"So, you leave the invalid to push you out to sea?" Mr. Carlisle teased as she climbed in.

"Whatever your skill with a fishing pole, you can at least manage this part of the process, can you not? It *will* take a great deal of strength. You will simply wait for—"

Mr. Carlisle gave a great push, and the boat slid forward, unsettling Judith from her seat and into the bottom of the boat.

Mr. Carlisle ran after the boat, making a great splash in the waves, then climbed in, causing it to rock from side to side. Wet from the thighs down, he steadied himself, then extended a hand toward Judith, who was staring at him with all the animus she could muster.

"You were saying?" He waited for her to place her hand in his, a wide smile on his face.

She didn't deign to reply to his provocation and accepted his hand begrudgingly.

He pulled her up with the same strength he had used to push the boat, and the force brought her right up against him. She stopped herself with her hands on his chest, but she needn't have, for he held her in place with a firm hand around the waist.

Too flustered for speaking and afraid he could feel her heartbeat with their sudden proximity, Judith pulled back in a hurry, sitting down on the board behind her in a less-than-elegant shuffle.

Mr. Carlisle sat down opposite her so that they faced one another, and he took the oars in hand. "Now, then. Where do we go, Miss Jardine?"

Hoping her cheeks weren't as hot as they felt, she cleared her throat. "Just past that cliff. The fish tend to gather in the pools nearby."

Mr. Carlisle seemed to need no instruction on the subject of rowing, and Judith secretly marveled at the speed with which he took them to their destination. She tried to keep her eyes trained on the water, even though they strayed time and again to the rhythmic movement of his shoulders. There was a contentment in his eyes, too, that struck her.

The sun was making its gradual progress toward the horizon, lengthening the shadow of the boat on the water, though the light hadn't yet taken on the golden glow Judith so loved.

"This will do," she said, feeling a heightened awareness of their solitude as they rounded the cliff, taking the beach they had departed from out of sight.

Mr. Carlisle laid down the oars and picked up a fishing pole. "Teach me, oh mistress."

She shot him an unamused look but complied, showing him how to thread the line through the loops on the pole, tie the hook to the line, and attach a lure. More than once, she found him looking at her rather than the pole or line. She tried to ignore it, though it made her fingers feel too large for their task and her cheeks warm.

"How very hot it is," she said after fumbling with the knot in the line.

Mr. Carlisle used his hands to fan her face, and she laughed, swatting them away.

"I *am* your servant, am I not?"

She shot a quick glance at him and took one of the poles in hand to occupy herself. "Your duties do not— however regrettably—include such a task."

He picked up the second pole, running a hand along it. "What makes you think everything I do for you is out of duty?"

He had made such flirtatious comments before, and they always left Judith feeling somewhat unhinged and flustered. She forced herself to wave them off, but she had seen in his eyes a growing glimmer of admiration—or perhaps something more.

Whatever it was, it wouldn't—it couldn't—survive the inevitable reckoning that the truth would bring.

"As for casting your line—"

In a deft movement, Mr. Carlisle whipped his rod in the air, sending the line sailing several fathoms away.

She stared at him, and he glanced at her.

"Was that wrong?" he asked.

"No, but . . . well, it was very disobliging of you. You might have at least waited for me to explain it so I could attribute your success to my instruction."

He laughed. "How *do* you know how to fish? Is that something most young ladies are practiced at?"

"Playing the pianoforte, stitching a sampler, catching and cleaning a fish," she said. The sound of his laugh gave her just as much pleasure as did her line reaching nearly as far as his. "I am not what one might call an *accomplished young lady*. George taught me to fish when I was here for Charlie's birth."

He pulled his line back in and recast it. "Surely, fishing is a more valuable accomplishment than stitching a sampler? Unless, of course, someone has found a way to subsist entirely on samplers, in which case London might be fed for years."

She laughed and looked at him thoughtfully. "And what do *you* know of London and Society?"

He glanced at her and shrugged as he pulled in his line. "Nothing, really."

"As much as you know of anything, then," she teased. "Have none of your memories returned?" Why did she feel such anxiety to hear the answer?

He looked her in the eye for a moment, then shook his head, and they fished in silence for a time, the only sounds the water lapping gently against the wood and the *plop* of their lines dropping into the water as Judith sat with troubling thoughts of what the future held.

Mr. Carlisle was the first to catch anything—a mackerel—and Judith tried to rein in her surprise.

"Beginner's luck." He grimaced as he pulled the fish from the line and set it in the bucket.

"Remembering Mr. Higgins?"

"Always," he said.

Judith managed to catch another mackerel shortly after, and Mr. Carlisle a second, after which a lull occurred. They sat in silence some of the time, but it was a peaceful silence rather than an awkward one, and Judith sighed contentedly as she took in the view around them.

"This is my favorite time of day," she said.

"Is it?" He looked at her with eyes slightly narrowed—sincere interest reflected in them.

"The water almost glows orange and, on a day like today, it is calm enough that it sparkles as it moves. There is nothing like it."

He gazed out at the vista around them. "I think you are right." Silence reigned for a moment. "Thank you."

She frowned and glanced at him as she readjusted the hook on her line. "For what?"

His gaze rested on her, soft and warm like the glow of the water. "For everything, Miss Jardine. For tending to me in my injuries, for giving me a place to recover, for sleeping in that miserable closet"—he smiled ruefully—"for being patient with me in my ineptitude. Not every mistress would do as much."

She looked away. "I am not your mistress, James."

"Not in a strict sense of the word, no."

Not in *any* sense of the word, she wanted to say.

He glanced at her with an amused smile. "Do you always turn off compliments and thanks when they are offered?"

"No," she said with a hint of defensiveness and even less persuasiveness.

He raised a brow at her, drawing his line back in. "I don't believe you."

"Well, you are wrong not to."

"Am I? Let us see about that." He set down his fishing pole and turned toward her purposefully.

"What are you doing?" she asked warily.

"Putting your assertion to the test. Let us see if you *can* accept a compliment—if you can look me in the eye and simply accept it rather than make some witty retort."

Judith scoffed and looked away. She should put Mr. Carlisle in his place. But that was the tricky thing about the situation she had created—what *was* his place? Her heart needed the protection afforded by insisting on a servant-mistress relationship, but her conscience balked at the lie.

Her hand was taken up, and she whipped her head around.

"There," he said as her eyes met his. He held her gaze as he took the rod from her hands and set it down next to his own.

She wanted to look away, but his eyes kept her there,

rooting her like an anchor. She expected to see teasing there, but instead, she saw sincerity and the admiration that so terrified her—terrified her for how much she wanted it to be real, for it not to crumble the moment Mr. Carlisle realized where he truly stood in relation to her and what she had done to him.

"You are the most extraordinary woman I have ever met," he said.

Her first impulse was to turn away, but Mr. Carlisle had anticipated it, and his hold on her hand tightened, reminding her of what she was tasked with doing. She gritted her teeth and fixed her eyes on him.

"You hold others at a distance with your wit and sarcasm," he said, "but you cannot hide the heart behind. It is softer and kinder than any I have ever encountered."

To her dismay, tears began to well in her eyes, and she turned her head away. "Says the man with no memories."

He laughed and put a hand to her cheek, guiding it to face him again. "You truly *cannot* do it, can you? Why is that?"

She blinked quickly. "Perhaps I doubt the sincerity of the compliments being offered." It was true, in part. She didn't doubt that he meant them now, in this moment. She merely doubted they would survive the return of his memory.

His brows knit together, and he searched her face, his own lit from behind with a sunny halo. "Then allow me to reassure you." He moved closer, taking her other cheek in hand, the intent in his eyes clear.

Judith should have pulled back immediately, but her heart revolted. It wanted the reassurance he was offering, and she shut her eyes. The boat listed gently, and she grasped his wrists to steady her. The touch of his lips was felt first on her own—soft, warm, unlike anything she had ever experienced. But its effects rippled out over her skin, down her back, and deep inside her—everywhere. She let go of his wrists, reaching her own hands around his neck, pulling him closer. The truth she had been holding in, all of the feelings she had been suppressing, demanded escape through the only medium offered to her, and Mr. Carlisle responded in kind, as if he had only been waiting for her invitation to give more.

One of his hands left her cheek, and she felt it next on her waist, pulling her nearer. The boat rocked with the shift, unsettling them, and Judith's eyes flew open. She broke away, reaching for stability on the sides of the boat.

CHAPTER TWELVE

J ames gripped the rim of the boat with one hand and steadied Miss Jardine with the other. She was staring at him, dismay building in her wide eyes.

Had he been wrong to kiss her? If so, he had never wanted so badly to be wrong again—and again. He didn't know what had motivated her to take him in and convince him he was a servant, but he knew her well enough to know she was regretting it. And whatever doubt there might have been in his mind about the nature of his feelings for Miss Jardine, it had slowly crumbled over the last few days.

But her eyes were full of such doubt now, and he felt guilt ripple and build inside him as he wondered what she was thinking, what she wanted.

"We should go," she said.

"But . . . we have only caught three fish."

"It will be enough. I am not hungry."

He watched her for another moment. "Miss Jardine," he said. "Forgive me—"

"No." She looked at him and smiled, but it was a counterfeit smile. "There is nothing to forgive. Here, allow me to row us to shore. You should not be exerting yourself so much. You are still injured, after all."

He grimaced and reached for the oars. She clearly did not wish to speak of the kiss. "I am fully capable of rowing, Miss Jardine."

James wondered if they might pass the time it took to reach the shore in utter silence, but what happened was worse. Miss Jardine kept up a monologue full of polite but vacuous remarks, while James only responded when a response was required of him. His mind was too full for anything more.

His heart urged him to tell her the truth—to tell her what he knew. But what would happen? The entire world they had constructed over the past week—absurd and ludicrous as it was—would shatter instantly.

I feel much safer with him here . . . Just a few more days, Judy. Those had been Mrs. Bradford's words. They needed him, servant or not. And he was not fool enough to think Miss Jardine would let him stay once the whole truth was laid before her. She had far too much pride for that.

When they reached the shore, he jumped out of the boat and into the chill water as he pulled the vessel onto the sand. The afternoon's glowing, orange hues had given way to ambers and deep reds as the sun settled on the horizon. Miss Jardine's talkativeness seemed to have dissipated with their arrival on shore, and after putting the boat in its place, their walk to the cottage was undertaken in silence.

But James couldn't pretend nothing had happened, and as they set the equipment back in place, he finally spoke.

"Miss Jardine, I cannot let things lie so easily as you."

"James, please," she said, shaking her head. "*Please* do so for my sake. I shall not tell my sister what happened, but if you insist on speaking of it, I shall have no choice."

He stared at her. She was threatening him with dismissal—dismissal from a fictitious position.

"You kissed me back." He couldn't stop himself.

She swallowed. "You are mistaken. Now, please. Say nothing more on the subject." She turned and walked to the cottage, disappearing through the door with only the briefest of glances at James.

⁂

JAMES DIDN'T EAT DINNER. HE SPENT THE EVENING cleaning and made do with a cup of ale at the table after the others had retired to bed and the house was dark and silent. The table was still laid, the dirty dishes before him, and a single candle lighting the room. There had been no time to clean the fish upon their arrival at the cottage, so they had been cooked whole.

One of the three plates contained the better part of a fish—picked at but largely uneaten. James had no doubt that it belonged to Miss Jardine. The head was intact, and the eye stared forward grotesquely, reminding James forcibly of Miss Garrett. He shuddered.

Tomorrow was the date of his expected meeting with Miss Garrett's father, and James found himself at a crossroads. He had been running from his life since his memories had returned, but he could only run for so long—particularly when he wasn't certain of his destination.

That he had fallen in love with Judith Jardine was no longer deniable—and in a shockingly short amount of time. That she returned at least some of his regard, he didn't doubt. But she was resisting it, and James could only assume it was her conscience that held her back. So, why the ruse?

His stomach rumbled, and he stared at the fish on Miss Jardine's plate, considering whether he should finish it off. Its juices glistened in the candlelight. It looked even less appetizing than had the fish at the dinner he had attended in—

He stilled.

The dinner. Fish juice.

His eyes widened, still fixed on the half-eaten fish as flutters of memories flapped around elusively in his head.

The woman beside him at dinner—the one he had hardly spoken with due to Miss Garrett's incessant talking. She had spilled on him, and he had nearly vomited, goaded beyond endurance by the sequence of undesirable events that night—until he had seen his opportunity to escape the dinner he had regretted almost since arriving at it.

He shut his eyes, trying to recapture the face of the woman beside him. It couldn't possibly be. Could it? She had told him her name at one point, hadn't she? She had, for he had elicited laughs from the table when, in his aggravation, he had turned her name into a joke.

Miss Sardine.

JAMES PERFORMED HIS DUTIES IN THE MORNING WITH almost more impatience than he could manage to contain. But despite the fact that he could hear the sounds of her movement within, Miss Jardine was slow to leave her bedchamber. She was still inside when the front door opened, and a man stepped into the house.

Kneeling at the hearth, James stared up at him, taking in the man's large girth and the way he looked on James with an expression of confusion.

"Who are you?" the man asked, eyes taking in James's task.

James stood just as Mrs. Bradford stepped into the room, followed by a toddling Charlie. She rushed toward the man. "George!"

Mr. Bradford wrapped his arms around his wife, and they kissed. James looked away out of politeness, feeling a little surge of envy. Charlie was anxious for the embrace to end, though, and Mr. Bradford picked him up with a laugh, planting a kiss on the boy's round cheek before turning to James again.

"Who is this?"

Mrs. Bradford looked at James with a great deal of anxiety in her eyes. "Oh," she said with a nervous laugh, "that is James. Come set your things down, George, and I shall explain it all." She ushered him out of the room with a firm hand, and James was left to himself again, smiling wryly. Mr. Bradford was clearly not complicit in the ruse.

As for James, he was suddenly deprived of his final excuse for staying; he was no longer needed in the Bradford household. His head whipped around at the sound of a door opening, and Miss Jardine appeared in the corridor, eyes sweeping the area. But the door to Mr. and Mrs. Bradford's bedchamber was closed.

Miss Jardine walked toward James. "Did I hear George?"

He nodded, feeling a great deal of nerves now that the opportunity he had been waiting for was finally before him. "He just returned. Went to set his things down and speak with your sister." He dusted off his hands and swallowed. "Could I speak with you outside, Miss Jardine?"

She looked at him with wariness.

"It is important," he said.

She gave a quick nod.

He opened the door for her, and she thanked him curtly, stepping into the refreshing morning air and walking the short path that led to the main road. She extended a brief greeting to a man driving a donkey cart there. Her arms were at her sides, somewhat rigid, and her fingers fiddled with her skirts.

"Miss Jardine," James said, his mouth feeling dry.

She turned toward him abruptly. "Let me speak first."

James frowned, looking at her intently. Was she going to tell him the truth? She *had* told her sister that she would only wait until Mr. Bradford returned. "I—"

"Hallo there!" The shout was nearly drowned out by the sound of horse hooves and carriage wheels, which soon decreased in volume, then stopped.

James turned toward the newly arrived chaise as the door opened, and a man stepped out—Philip Langham.

CHAPTER THIRTEEN

J udith couldn't move. The stranger who had just appeared could not have come at a more inopportune time. It had taken her all night to garner the courage to tell Mr. Carlisle everything—the courage to accept that, whatever visions of possibility she had created, they would only ever be dreams. George's arrival had decided things.

"I am devilishly relieved to find you here," the stranger said to Mr. Carlisle. "The first report I followed turned out to be a hum! I admit, I had my doubts when the fellow spoke of a man without a memory, but—" He clapped a hand on Mr. Carlisle's shoulder and surveyed his clothing with obvious distaste. "Good heavens, Carlisle. What in heaven's name happened to you?" He looked at him through narrowed eyes. "You *do* remember me, don't you?"

Judith's gaze shifted rapidly between the two men. Mr. Carlisle was watching her, though, a somber expression on his face. His gaze lingered on her for a moment as he turned to the man by his side.

"What are you doing here, Langham?" Mr. Carlisle asked.

Judith's heart plummeted. He knew the man. His memories were returning, and she hadn't been able to explain everything.

"What do you *think* I'm doing here?" the man called Langham said as he laughed. "People had begun to think you dead. But I knew better. Knew you didn't want to offer for the Garrett girl—figured you had found something more entertaining." He glanced at Judith finally, chuckling again. "And all this time, you have been having a little dalliance with Miss Sardine, of all people!"

Judith stiffened, and her face flooded with color on hearing the nickname. She looked to Mr. Carlisle, and the guilt in his expression answered the questions she had only just begun to ask herself. He *knew*. He knew everything.

"Your father will be mad as fire when he knows the truth of it, I can tell you that much. Come." Mr. Langham took Mr. Carlisle's arm. "You can stay with me at the Red Lion"—he glanced at Mr. Carlisle's clothing again and shuddered with disgust—"and we can find you a tailor until you return to London."

"Stop, Langham," Mr. Carlisle said, not budging from his place.

Mr. Langham paused, and his brows shot up.

Mr. Carlisle gently took his arm from the man's grasp. "I am not coming with you."

"Eh?" Mr. Langham gave an uncomfortable laugh.

"I am in the middle of a conversation just now. You will have to wait."

"No," Judith said in a clipped voice. "We have finished our conversation. You should go."

Mr. Carlisle turned to her, searching her face, a frown on his brow. "Miss Jardine."

Mr. Langham covered a chuckle, and Judith's nostrils flared, well aware that her name was a source of amusement to him.

"You knew!" she shot at Mr. Carlisle, unable to contain herself any longer. "You knew this entire time!" What did it matter if Mr. Langham heard what she said? She was done caring for the opinion of such people.

"No," Mr. Carlisle said, coming closer to her and reaching out a hand. "I didn't. I—"

She stepped backward. "Stay away from me. I am nothing but sport to you—a joke from the very first time we met. And you . . ." She swallowed. "I can only hope everyone in England comes to learn the sort of person you are."

She turned on her heel, but he grabbed her hand, keeping her from going. Mr. Langham was watching with wide eyes, but he seemed to come out of his staring trance, clearing his throat and hurriedly stepping up into the carriage. "I'll just be in here, dear boy!"

Mr. Carlisle gave no indication of hearing his friend. "You are not sport to me, Miss Jardine."

"Am I not?" She pulled her hand away. "Miss Sardine has not been your *entertainment?*" She nodded at the carriage Mr. Langham was inside.

"No! I should have told you when my memories returned, but . . ." His shoulders came up. "I didn't want it to end—I wanted more time with you."

She pulled her hand away, shaking her head. "I do not believe a word you say. You have been lying this entire time."

Mr. Carlisle blinked. "*I* have been lying? And what of you? You convinced me I was a *servant.* You had me cleaning fish and the privy, sleeping in quarters one might expect to find in gaol. And for what? Revenge? Because I made a silly comment at a dinner?"

"You think that is all it was?" she cried, incredulous. "A silly comment? You were the most ill-mannered *gentleman* I have ever come across."

His eyes widened, and she could see that her insult had landed. "Forgive me if I have not lived up to the standards of all the gentlemen you have undoubtedly encountered in a place like *this.*" He gestured to the house.

Rage ran hot through Judith's veins. "Oh, yes. You made your prejudices against those less fortunate than you quite clear at dinner. But what claim have *you* to the title of gentleman when you ignored me for the entirety of dinner, left me to fend for myself instead of serving me any food, and, as if that was not enough, made a laughing-stock of me, ruining any chance I had at a match?" Her jaw hardened, but she couldn't fend off the tears much longer. "You deserved every moment here, and I hope it serves you—and Miss Garrett—well. Please offer her the compliments of Miss *Sardine*."

She wheeled around and stalked toward the path they had taken to the beach just the day before, refusing to wipe the tears that slipped onto her cheeks until she was no longer in Mr. Carlisle's line of sight, her body trembling with anger and feeling.

The path finally sloped downward, and with a quick, bleary glance over her shoulder, she sank onto the sand and surrendered to emotion.

CHAPTER FOURTEEN

James watched Miss Jardine disappear behind the hill that led down to the beach, his chest rising and falling rapidly. He was angry. He was confused. He was guilty. And he was heartbroken. He had anticipated the encounter would be unpleasant, but this? He had not anticipated this.

"Carlisle?" Langham's voice was tentative coming through the chaise window, which had been open the entire time. Langham had heard everything. He and the postilion waiting by the horses for his orders, who fiddled awkwardly with the bridle of a horse.

"It seems my timing has been rather unfortunate," Langham said, clenching his teeth. "I can return later, if you would like. Or not."

"No," James said, not allowing himself a look at the house or the spot where Miss Jardine had disappeared.

She had been quite clear what she thought of him. There was nothing for him here. "I am coming with you."

He climbed into the chaise and sank down into the seat across from Langham, who watched him for a moment, then hit a fist against the roof.

The chaise pulled forward, and they rode in silence for some time, James occupied with unhappy thoughts, and Langham no doubt feeling awkward at the strange situation he had happened upon.

After ten minutes, though, Langham cleared his throat. "Forgive me, Carlisle, but . . . what the devil just happened?"

James let out a sigh and let his head fall back against the tufted seat back. He shook it from side to side, wishing he could forget all of it, unable to put it into words.

"You must be ready to give *some* sort of explanation to people, Carlisle. And better you sort through what to say with me than bumbling through it with your father or Miss Garrett."

Miss Garrett's name made James cringe. But Langham was right. He had decisions to make, and with the bundle of emotions he was still feeling, he was bound to make a muddle of it if he didn't think things through first.

"Start at the beginning, man," Langham said. "Start when I last saw you—before you decided to dress like a dashed hot air balloon."

THE CHAISE SLOWED AS IT PASSED BY ANOTHER
equipage, and James shrugged his shoulders, having come
to the point of the story where Langham had arrived. He
had glazed over a few details—his feelings for Miss
Jardine, in particular—but Langham had the long and
short of it, at least.

Langham stared at him. "You fell in love with her?
With Miss Sardine?"

James's brows snapped together. "Don't, Langham.
Don't call her that." He looked through the window at the
shrubs that lined the road. "I never knew what effect those
words would have."

"Effect?" Langham laughed. "They gave everyone a
great laugh. Very clever, it was."

"And thoughtless and cruel."

Langham looked at him under furrowed brows. "You
really do love her, then?"

"What does it matter?"

"Don't be a fool, Carlisle. If you love the girl, what in
heaven's name are you doing in here with me?"

"It doesn't matter, because she doesn't believe me,
Langham. She thinks it's all been for sport—a great lie—
and I cannot blame her."

"No one is asking you to blame her, you oaf,"
Langham said impatiently. "I'm telling you to *make her
believe you.*"

James grimaced. "And who's to say that would change
anything? She called me"—he let out a frustrated breath as
he tried to remember what exactly she had said.

"The most ill-mannered gentleman she had ever come across," Langham supplied.

James shot him a glare. "Yes, *thank you.*"

"Don't look daggers at me. *I* didn't say it." Langham tapped his finger on the hat in his lap. "Listen, Carlisle. If you want a guarantee that she'll have you, I can't give it to you. Can't say I'm an expert on the topic, but love is always a risk, isn't it?"

James leaned forward, resting his elbows on his knees and clasping his hands in front of his mouth. "Even if she would have me, what of my father?"

Langham waved a dismissive hand. "I imagine he will be so happy to know you are alive *and* choosing to marry, he will overlook your slight to Miss Garrett."

"It is not a slight," James said testily. "She is to receive an offer from Sir William."

"True. And that *is* a good match, I say, if only for the fact that she will be able to stare to her heart's content while Sir William is none the wiser. Everyone knows the man is blind—everyone except him, of course."

James could feel his hands sweating and his heart hammering harder and harder as he stared at the chaise floor. Every second he hesitated put more distance between him and Judith, and he felt every inch in his soul.

"Stop the chaise," he said softly.

Nothing happened, and he looked up at his friend.

"Hmm?" Langham said, feigning deafness. "Did you say something?"

"Stop the chaise," James said louder.

Langham smiled. "Confidence, Carlisle. Confidence is key." He hit his fist against the roof. "Now, let us catch you a sardine."

CHAPTER FIFTEEN

Judith's arms were wrapped around her knees, and the shoulders of her dress were wet from using them to dry her tears. The tears had stopped, though, and the trails on her cheeks had dried with the sea breeze.

Watching the waves roll in and out, in and out, calmed her, helping her collect the pieces which had come apart in front of Mary's house. Her heart still ached with a sense of loss—not all of her attempts to distance herself from Mr. Carlisle had managed to prevent that.

Nor did knowing that he hadn't been honest with her act as a salve on her conscience, for she knew that he was not the only one in the wrong. Focusing on his mistakes did not erase her own. And it had been the knowledge of her own culpability which had made her temper flare more easily than it otherwise would have, leading her to speak the unkind words she had spewed.

Mr. Carlisle's incivility had begotten the whole situation, certainly, but upon reflection, Judith had to admit that her own behavior was the more reprehensible.

A breeze blew up some of the sand around her feet and made the reeds behind her rustle musically. She glanced at them, and her gaze settled on the boat hiding amongst them.

A few residual tears obscured her vision as thoughts of the kiss she had shared with Mr. Carlisle crept into her tired mind. She shut her eyes for a moment, remembering how it had felt to be held by him and, even more importantly, the look in his eyes before he had kissed her.

All of it had been wrapped up in lies.

"Miss Jardine?"

She jumped at the unexpected voice and hurriedly wiped the tears from her eyes before turning.

Mr. Carlisle stood at the top of the sandy slope, his oversized shirt billowing with the wind in a way Judith might have found amusing yesterday. But just now, it made her heart ache.

He stepped down the slope toward her, boots sinking into the deep sand.

"What do you want, Mr. Carlisle?" she asked in a weary voice as she turned back toward the water.

He said nothing, merely sitting down beside her and putting his arms around his knees just as hers were. They sat in silence, listening to the waves and the grass rustling, watching the white sail of a boat in the distance.

"I am sorry, Miss Jardine," Mr. Carlisle finally said. "For so many things."

She stared straight ahead, even though she wanted to see his face again—to look into his eyes and see whether the sincerity she had seen there in the boat yesterday had been imagined, or if it was still there. If she didn't see him, perhaps she could forget how much she cared for him.

"I am sorry for being so ill-mannered at that dinner. I was so focused on deterring the woman I didn't want that I neglected the only woman I ever *could* want."

Unable to bear it any longer, Judith looked at him, her heart throbbing at the sight. If ever a man had meant what he said, James Carlisle did so now. His eyes said it all.

"I am sorry for the terrible, thoughtless joke I made about your name. And I am sorry for not being honest with you when I began to remember things."

She had seen him degrade himself countless times over the past ten days, but none of that had been as satisfying as she had imagined it would be. His apology, though, filled her in ways she had never anticipated.

She took in a deep breath. "And *I* am sorry. For not being honest with you from the beginning as I should have been." She forced herself to look him in the eye, to face up to her decisions.

"Why *did* you do it?" he asked. "What I mean to say is, well"—the corner of his mouth turned up—"what in heaven's name were you thinking?"

She thought back on that day—on the moment when she had made that small decision that had grown into such a complicated lie. "It was a silly, impulsive decision," she said. "I never meant for it to go on so long. I merely wanted to teach you a lesson for an hour or two. But then Mr. Sharp forbade me from saying anything that might overset you, or from forcing your memories onto you, and" —she lifted her shoulders helplessly—"I didn't know what to do."

He gave a half-smile that flipped her heart. "Your obedience to Mr. Sharp is inspiring, if somewhat unexpected."

She turned herself toward him more, needing to explain. "He told me the most horrid stories, threatening me with the prospect of driving you to insanity—of sending you to Bedlam, where you would die a madman."

"Good heavens," Mr. Carlisle said with a laugh.

She reached for a handful of sand, letting it slip through her fingers. "I thought surely your memories would return when you began to take on the role of servant. But they did not." She looked at him with a frown. "Or so I thought."

He smiled apologetically.

"Why did you not tell me?" she asked.

"I very nearly did—almost boxed your ears. But I decided against it, for a number of reasons. The reason I tried most to believe was simply my wish to escape the duties that awaited me as James Carlisle."

She narrowed her eyes at him. "Surely, those duties were not more unpleasant than cleaning the privy."

He laughed, and Judith watched the reflection of the bright water in his eyes with longing. She had never denied his charm or attraction, but to her, he had never possessed more of either than in this moment, with the sea in his eyes, George's shirt drowning him, and a laugh on his lips.

"That is up for debate," he said. "But it was not the only reason I stayed—and it was certainly not what kept me here. As I look back now, I can admit that the real reason for playing along with the ruse was"—he let out a breath through his nose and looked at her—"you."

Her heart skipped a few beats.

"I wanted to understand you," he said, "to puzzle you out. I wanted to be with you."

She searched his eyes for a moment, then looked away, but he guided her face back with a hand. "Don't turn away, Judith. I need you to believe me. I know I have no right to your trust after everything, but I am asking for it anyway."

She shut her eyes. "I am sorry, James. But I find it inconceivable that you—a man so accustomed to being served that you must hardly notice the people who serve you—chose to continue being a servant just to spend time with *me*." She shook her head and swallowed, but he kept his hand on her cheek, and all she wanted was to nestle into it.

He came to kneel before her, taking her other cheek in hand. "Please look at me, Judith."

She slowly opened her eyes, and he held her gaze intently. "I will be your servant for the rest of my life, Judith, if only it means I get to love you." He rested his forehead against hers. "Please let me."

She shut her eyes, savoring the impossible moment, feeling the warmth of his head resting against hers and his breath grazing her nose and tickling her lips.

"If you still do not believe me, only feel how my heart beats for you," he said softly, taking her hand and placing it on his chest. A quick pattering tapped against her hand, a language all its own, and she lifted her chin, catching his lips with hers.

He responded willingly, pulling her closer until she lost her balance, and they tumbled backward onto the sand. He held her against him, laughing, and they rolled down the slope until the ground leveled out. She found herself on her back, looking into the face hovering above her, lit from behind like it had been in the boat yesterday, gazing at her with tenderness and the smile she had come to crave.

He dipped down for a kiss, and, pulling him closer, she forced him to roll to the side, their lips still locked together. Sand sprinkled from her hair down into her dress and stays, stopping where James's hand pressed against the small of her back. She pulled away, looking down on him now from above, admiring the way his dark eyes and hair contrasted with the sandy backdrop.

"When *did* your memories return?" she asked.

His mouth twisted to the side guiltily, and he waited before responding. "The night we cleaned the fish."

Her jaw dropped open, and he recoiled slightly, as though afraid of what she might do.

"That long ago?" she said in dismay.

He nodded, apology written on his face. "Mr. Sharp's newspaper must have slipped out of his bag when he came to visit the second time. There happened to be an advertisement within requesting information regarding my whereabouts. It all began to come back when I saw my name." He grimaced. "Can you ever forgive me?"

She considered him through narrowed eyes. "A few more nights in the closet ought to balance the books."

He reached a hand up, threading his fingers through her hair and looking at her in a way that made her heart thump.

"A small sacrifice," he said. "I have become somewhat fond of it, you know."

"What? Of the closet?"

He nodded. "It is full of thoughts of you."

"And bruised heads and pokey straw," she said with a laugh. "Besides, it wouldn't take very many thoughts of me to fill *that* space. I begin to think you have overestimated your affection for me."

He guided her head down until their lips just brushed. "Then allow me to reassure you, my love."

EPILOGUE

J udith and James walked arm-in-arm along the damp
sands of the beach at Brighton, waves threatening
their feet again and again, only to withdraw. Judith
looked to the north, letting her gaze travel along the row of
townhouses that lined the coast.

She had been hesitant to come to Brighton after their
wedding, but experiencing the seaside town as a new bride
was entirely different than experiencing it as Miss Jardine
less than three months ago. With the arrival of autumn
temperatures, many of Society had begun to trickle out of
the seaside town. Judith preferred it a little quieter and
calmer. She enjoyed her promenades with James when
there were fewer people to greet.

She was also happy to be in such close proximity to
Mary and their new baby girl, Sarah. George had received
a new position on an estate just north of Brighton, and
things were looking up for the Bradford family.

More than anything, though, Judith no longer felt like an imposter here. She didn't wonder anymore whether she fit into Society. She and James belonged together, and that was all that mattered to her. She belonged where he belonged.

Two people approached from the opposite direction, and Judith and James slowed once they were recognized.

"Carlisle," Mr. Langham said as he came upon them. He walked with a woman of middling age whom, given their similarity in appearance, Judith took to be his mother.

James tipped his hat. "Good day, Langham. Mrs. Langham."

"Mother," Mr. Langham said, "allow me to introduce you to Mrs. Carlisle—formerly known as Miss Sardine."

James cleared his throat significantly, looking anything but amused.

"Miss *Jardine*," Langham corrected himself.

Judith laughed softly and curtsied to Mrs. Langham.

"The notorious Miss Sardine," Mrs. Langham said, but her smile was so warm and her voice so kind that they robbed the words of any offense. "How lovely to finally meet you. I have heard so much about you."

"Oh dear," Judith said with a nervous laugh.

"I just saw your father yesterday, Mr. Carlisle," Mrs. Langham continued, "and he wasted no time informing us of his son's recent marriage."

Judith glanced at James, raising her brows. James's

mother had welcomed Judith with open arms, but his father had taken more time to come around to the match. James smiled down at her, as if to say, *I told you so.* He had been adamant about two things when they had become engaged: first, that his father would be powerless against Judith's charms, and second, that he didn't give a fig for what his father thought anyway.

"You heard about Sir William and Miss Garrett, I imagine?" Mr. Langham asked.

"Married last week, were they not?" James replied.

Mrs. Langham smiled and nodded. "I met them near the Pavilion just yesterday, arm in arm. Very much in love —Miss Garrett could not keep her eyes from her new husband."

Mr. Langham coughed, though it sounded suspiciously like a laugh.

"I can only imagine," James said, holding Judith all the closer.

THEY PARTED FROM THE LANGHAMS SHORTLY AFTER, and James sighed as they continued their walk.

"I apologize for Langham," he said. "He can be the greatest of dolts."

"It is quite all right," Judith said, smiling. "I have embraced the name, you know. I find it amusing now."

He looked at her through narrowed eyes. "Do you?"

She nodded.

"And what of Brighton?" he asked. "Do you dislike it here?"

She stopped and took in a breath of fresh sea air, shaking her head. "I quite like it now."

He came to stand before her, playing with her bonnet ribbon, which rippled in the wind. "I am glad to hear that. I thought perhaps your memories of the place had ruined it for you forever."

"I thought so, too. But even those memories are happy now, thanks to you." She took his hand, holding it within hers. "It is funny how that happens, isn't it? Our memories are not really fixed. They take on new shape as the future takes form, and even the worst ones can evolve into something happy, if only they have guided us to a joyful present."

He brought one of her hands to his lips and kissed it fervently. "A joyful present, indeed. I love you, Judith." He wrapped his arms around her waist. "*Miss Sardine.*"

"And I you, Mr. Carlisle."

He smiled softly. "Your servant."

THE END

OTHER TITLES BY MARTHA KEYES

A Conspiratorial Courting (Book 2)

A Matchmaking Mismatch (Book 3)

Standalone Titles

Host for the Holidays (Christmas Escape Series)

A Suitable Arrangement (Castles & Courtship Series)

Goodwill for the Gentleman (Belles of Christmas 2)

The Christmas Foundling (Belles of Christmas: Frost Fair 5)

The Highwayman's Letter (Sons of Somerset 5)

Of Lands High and Low

Mishaps & Memories (Timeless Regency Collection)

The Road through Rushbury (Seasons of Change 1)

Eleanor: A Regency Romance

ABOUT THE AUTHOR

Whitney Award-winning Martha Keyes was born, raised, and educated in Utah—a home she loves dearly but also dearly loves to escape to travel the world. She received a BA in French Studies and a Master of Public Health, both from Brigham Young University.

Her route to becoming an author was full of twists and turns, but she's finally settled into something she loves. Research, daydreaming, and snacking have become full-time jobs, and she couldn't be happier about it. When she isn't writing, she is honing her photography skills, looking for travel deals, and spending time with her family. She lives with her husband and twin boys in Vineyard, Utah.

Printed in Great Britain
by Amazon